UNINVITED GUESTS

UNINVITED
GUESTS

JANE
GILLESPIE

JANUS PUBLISHING COMPANY
London, England

First published in Great Britain 1994
by Janus Publishing Company
Duke House, 37 Duke Street
London W1M 5DF

ISBN 1 85756 151 1

Printed and bound in England by
Antony Rowe Ltd, Chippenham, Wiltshire

1

A newly built terrace of large houses in a residential part of Bristol was now occupied, and even in the rainy twilight of a spring day looked pleasant and neat, with freshly painted railings and lights in several windows. Only the last house in the terrace was still in some disarray; its owner had begun to construct a portico at its doorway and apparently meant to build an arched entrance to a stable yard behind the house; blocks of stone and heaped cobbles scattered the area. The owner himself was at his desk indoors, absorbed in calculations attendant on his plans. Papers, some crumpled or scribbled over, heaped his desk; some he clustered into untidy heaps and some he cast, muttering, on the floor. From the titles of these papers they were bills from builders, glaziers, lawyers – and bootmakers, farriers and many others besides. The houseowner – a sturdy gentleman of middle years – was too much absorbed in his reckonings to hear sounds of arrival from below. When a servant opened the door of the room he growled: 'Go away.'

'Mrs Firth is here, sir.'

'Well tell *her* to go away.'

The command came too late; a lady, having pursued the servant upstairs, was already in the room, throwing off her damp travelling cloak and declaring: 'I came straight to you!' She tossed her cloak to the servant and bade him: 'Have them take my boxes up.'

'Boxes! Are you intending to stay?' protested the sturdy gentleman, clapping both fists to his brow.

'What else? Where else could I go? You are my own brother – and George has cast me out of the house. My own sister's husband has insulted me and turned me away like a servant.'

'Has he, by G——?' said her brother, roused to indignation. 'Insulted you, has he?' He leapt up and flourished his hand as if pointing a duelling pistol. 'I shall call him out, the base hound. Did Anne not prevent him? Cast you out, did he?'

His sister, seating herself at the fireside, replied: 'Oh, you know Anne – she could not cast a . . . cockroach out of the house. Nor need you challenge George, do not be so full of swagger.'

John for a moment redirected his forefinger as if he considered the alternative of shooting his sister; then dropping his hand he admitted:

'I suppose nothing would be gained by thrashing the man. He has his uses. He is, after all, paying for your son's education.'

'Roland will repay him – every penny!' Mrs Firth exclaimed.

'Brave words. But when will that be?' He shrugged, turning his chair and seating himself to face his sister. 'What is more, when will Roland take it upon himself to support his widowed mother?'

'Roland is still a child,' declared Mrs Firth, adding in a haughty tone: 'Nor do I consider myself relegated to the status of a widow.'

As her husband had died some ten years ago, it might have been supposed that she had by now recognised such a status; but her brother understood – as had always been evident – that Mrs Firth considered herself eligible for remarriage. Holding her hands to the fire she complained: 'It is cold in here. May we not have some tea?'

'Oh, please make free with my house,' said John with heavy irony. Standing, he kicked at the coals in the hearth. 'Where, by the way, is your precious Roland? Did George not turn him out too?'

'He is at Oxford, naturally,' and shrugging too, she murmured: 'George hardly sees him; nor do I. His face is always behind a book, if I do. And he spends all his vacations as a private tutor – somewhere.'

'Yes,' said John indifferently, 'Roland is a bore.'

Roland's mother did not contradict that; she glanced about her in a dejected manner. 'It grows dark; why not draw the curtains . . . I see you have no curtains; why not? My dear John, you have no notion of making a house habitable—'

'Then you will not be encouraged to stay here.'

'By *you* I see I shall not. However, I believe you will not be long here yourself.'

'What makes you think that?'

'I am told you are renting a mansion in the country for this summer,' Mrs Firth mentioned in a casual manner.

'I am – What? Who the d— told you such a tale?'

'Mama, of course. It was you who told her.'

'I told her nothing of the kind,' denied John, his tone loudly blustering. 'She must be growing senile—'

'If you condescended to visit her you would perceive that she is not. And we all allow for your practice of colouring up every tale you tell – in short, of boasting. For instance – you told us that *this* house was large and convenient and furnished by you at magnificent expense; and look at the muddle it is—'

'It is nothing of the kind. As soon as I have the stable block built – It will be splendid – If you did not come and interrupt when I am at work on my schemes . . .' He drew

7

breath, waved a hand and pursued: 'And if you do not care to stay here I shall not press you—'

'I hardly expected you to. But listen to me: Since I am for the present homeless – and since I do not believe even you could invent a country mansion – and since Mama, happy as she is to live with Maria and Charles, would welcome a rest and country air – it would seem to be in your power to show a little kindness at last to your own family. You have no wife or children of your own, and no obligations—'

John kicked again at the coals with a vigour that crumbled them to ash. 'If I have no wife of my own, is that a reason to load me with a houseful of widows? With all my schemes and projects that occupy my whole time—'

'Not to much purpose,' said Mrs Firth drily. 'And you squander enough money on your visits to Bath and London – and on renting mansions, if that turns out to mean merely a cottage—'

'I assure you,' said John, unguarded, 'the estate I have in mind is large and noble and of historic interest—'

'Then it will provide you with a chance to accept some of your family responsibilities.'

'Why, for G—'s sake?' shouted John. He added: 'I can see why George threw you out of his house.'

'I defy you to do the same to me. Now, explain to me where this estate of yours is, and what accommodation it offers.'

John pondered, scowling. He knew his eldest sister to be remorseless and relentless. After a while he admitted in a lower and unwilling voice:

'The situation there is not, in truth, quite as I described it to our mother. Of course I am doing the friend who owns it a great favour – which makes me the more obliged to behave with correctness and honour . . .' He adopted a more persuasive tone as he rehearsed inwardly the explanation that was being forced from him.

* * *

His small stature, as with many men so afflicted, required John to entertain a correspondingly high conceit of himself; he assumed a superior knowledge on any topic, from horse-flesh to finance, and let it be known that he was privy to the innermost secrets of all his wide circle of acquaintance. Should he encounter anyone better informed or more discreet than himself, he would extricate himself from such embarrassment by bluster or by avoidance; he was not easily abashed. It happened that recently he had set himself up as an authority on architecture and estate management, largely to oblige a friend whom he had met during the last several years on his annual visit to Bath.

'By G—, yes,' John told him. 'These old places are millstones round one's neck. Lord Grimley was telling me – you know him, of course? – that he has to spend thousands a year on upkeep – just to maintain it, you know, no thought of improvements – and even my own little property in Bristol – I swear, what I've spent on that already – it has been done in the best of taste, of course, but what I have had to pay those thieving builders – I have to watch them all the time . . .'

The friend in question knew John only slightly and, taken up with his own difficulties, was glad of a sympathetic listener. John's inquiries had revealed that this Colonel of a distinguished regiment had lost his father some five years ago; that the family possessed a valuable estate in Gloucestershire; that the Colonel had no interest in his inheritance, nor in country life; that his wife had less; but that the Colonel was being pressed to give his attention to his duty:

'. . . My duty, they say, to bury myself – My younger brother even thinks I should resign my commission and ape a country squire – Gad, leave all my London and army friends – What is more, I have two daughters to marry off – What chance would they have down in that backwater – And the steward whines away about the condition of the woodlands – Gad, do you know how many staff I have to pay there, just

9

to keep the dreary place going – And have I no *duty* to my regiment or to my family . . .?'

So he grumbled on, after a couple of bottles of wine, while John nodded and shook his head. John's own inquiries, pursued, confirmed what he knew of the Colonel's relatives: The officious younger brother, a clergyman, held a living some twenty miles distant from the estate; one sister, married to a Viscount, lived far away in Derbyshire; the Colonel's wife was a vain, extravagant woman whose only interest was in the gaieties of London or Bath; the two potentially marriageable daughters, now of an age to attend the public balls of Bath, were copies of their mother – pretty enough but giddy. John had had dealings at one time with the Colonel's late father, the General, and in his opinion the family might be still suffering the effects of the old brute's tyranny, relieved as they must be to be rid of him.

None of this did John apply to himself until, in pursuance of another of his ploys, he found himself forced to spend a night at a village inn close by the gates of the Colonel's domain. John had set out from Bath to sell his brand-new cabriolet and splendid thoroughbred horse to an acquaintance who had been tempted into offering a large price; but when a wheel fell off the cabriolet and the horse turned as fractious as an army mule, even John's excuses could not prevail; nor would his acquaintance offer a night's lodging; but on discovering his whereabouts, John felt that perhaps his luck had not deserted him. 'Why,' he declared to the landlord of the inn, 'had I known the district better, I could have lodged with another friend, my old comrade the Colonel.'

'The Colonel is from home, sir. Are you a friend of the family?'

'Lord, I have known them all my life. Frederick will be disappointed to have missed me.'

'You will not often find him here, sir. I think it is two – or more – years since he came.'

10

'He has told me that he is not fond of the place, yes. I knew it in the old General's day but have not been here since. It cannot be much changed?'

'As to that, sir, I dare say not, but it is a pity it should not be occupied, a grand old building like that.'

'It will fall to rack and ruin if it is not.'

'As to that, sir, it is well looked after. Mr Benson is a good and honest steward.'

'I am sure of it. And Frederick pays up – That is, funds are available for maintenance?'

As to that, said the landlord, he could not say, but probably the Colonel's lawyers dealt with Mr Benson – whom, if the gentleman wished to inquire, the gentleman might wish to meet?

The gentleman expressed himself glad to. 'Frederick would be grateful if, while I am in the district, I could gather some reassurance for him that all is in order.'

So it was that on the next morning Mr Benson and John carried out a tour of the premises. John – who had never been here before – was genuinely interested; the original buildings had been of a religious foundation and retained the title of an 'abbey'. Few of the ancient features remained, and a modern wing had replaced the side of the quadrangle that had contained monastic cells; but the whole had aspects of grandeur and antiquity that harmonised with the surroundings and had an impressive effect. The grounds were tastefully laid out, with many walled gardens and shrubberies. 'But,' as Mr Benson pointed out, 'the pineries and fruit gardens, as well as the outlying farm lands, need not be productively worked when the family is not resident.' Indeed there were patches of bare earth, however well raked, and empty dairy offices and stable yards. 'Were this mine,' John cried, with a sweeping gesture across the landscape, 'I could never bear to live elsewhere!'

This at last had a modifying effect on Mr Benson's attitude. He sighed. He bent to tug out a weed from the verge

of the carriageway. Twirling the weed between his fingers
he said in a burst: 'There is so *much* of it!'

'And a thankless work if the owner is always away.'

'I expect no thanks,' said Mr Benson hastily. 'But as you
can imagine, there is responsibility – I cannot always be
asking the Colonel whether to renew the lead in the window
of the great hall – or let the woodman fell trees whose
roots are raising the flagstones – They all appeal to me; the
authority is laid on me . . .'

'The other members of the family are no help?' hinted
John.

'Oh, the Reverend Henry – Mr Henry – visits when he
can; in the summer he brings his niece – a very pleasant
young lady,' Mr Benson put in, his expression softening.
'And Miss Eleanor – her Ladyship – is of course sympathetic;
but . . .' He shook his head, omitting any further reproach
of his employer.

John returned to Bath and at a propitious moment
approached the Colonel with a full report on his visit to the
Abbey. '—As I happened to be in the district.' The estate,
he declared, was a magnificent place; nowhere in the
country was like it; it deserved – and needed – the best of
attention. 'It would be criminal to let it go to rack and ruin.
Your steward there – Mr Benson – is a good sort of man but
the responsibility is too much for him – and your housekeeper Mrs What-was-it is getting old – I do not mean that
anyone is neglectful, but there is no one to take things fully
in hand and give the whole place a thorough tidying-up.
Now, if you could find someone who knew enough of such
things and could take command, it could all be rendered
impeccable in two or three months at most – As I have
mentioned, I have the experience – I wish I could make the
time to help you out . . .' He consulted a list from his pocket,
shaking his head. 'Yes; I made a few notes for your guidance
– let me see . . . Tree roots cracking the pavements – the
lead in the hall windows falling out – I suspect, even dry rot

in the splendid oak staircase . . . creeping mould in the unused glass-houses . . . a blocked drain in the stables that will flood the yards if we have rain . . . Weeds, even, growing in the driveway—'

'Oh, stop. What a tale of doom. I do not believe things can be as bad as that.'

'Then, do you go and see for yourself. When you do, I swear it, you will be horrified, and you will not be able to make yourself leave again until all these – and more, I am sure – grievous faults have been dealt with. I never in my life saw a place so much threatened when a little time and effort could save it – and a little money spent now will save you a cool fortune if you do not let the neglect continue . . .'

The Colonel was made uneasy. He had earnestly intended to spend at least a month of each summer at the Abbey, but in the five years of his ownership had achieved this only once. – But, two years ago, or was it three, surely the estate had not been threatened with such decrepitude? He consulted his wife. 'I ought to see for myself. This Thorpe exaggerates—'

'Oh, why should you suspect that? If he is so much interested, tell him to see to the matter himself.'

'I hardly know the man. He says he is much occupied, too, with his own concerns—'

'Pay him,' said his lady shrewdly. 'Anything, to save us the worry – and to avoid our going down to a ruinous old place when we might be in France with the Duchesnes. You might have some regard for my wishes. I did not marry you in order to spend my life under dry-rotted beams far from civilisation.'

It suited John very well to remove himself for a time from civilisation; when he returned from Bath to Bristol he was met by debts, unfinished building, and a threatened court case brought by the architects and residents of the new terrace, who claimed he had violated the regulations and lowered the tone of the area. His 'own concerns' did not

detain him when the Colonel offered him the task of saving
the Abbey from ruin; it seemed that John's position was
secured for the immediate future. What he had not
expected, or reckoned with, was that his widowed sister and
mother should uninvited accompany him. That Mrs Firth
had been cast out by her brother-in-law, he did not take
seriously; she quarrelled frequently with anyone who gave
refuge to her poverty. But she had always been able to bully
him and he could think of no escape.

2

Mrs Firth would have disallowed any such coarse word as 'bully' to describe her treatment of her brother, but she saw no reason to spare him, since he was responsible for her choice of husband and consequent poverty.

Her poverty afflicted her more grievously even than her widowhood. Her family was not wealthy, so her future was dependent on an early and provident marriage, an aim which she pursued with no advantages beyond beauty, high spirits and a private determination to marry quickly and to outshine her younger sisters. So during one season in Bath she formed an engagement with a young clergyman, off whom she as quickly cooled when he was offered only a ill-paid living; she fancied herself favoured by another young man of fortune who cooled off her – Then, disappointed and anxious, she tolerated the attentions of a handsome but frivolous Horace Firth, in order to escape the disgrace of appearing partnerless in the ballroom. It was her brother John – always inquisitive, always gossiping – who told her:

'I know he is a nitwit, but do you know who his father is? He is the owner of the Regent Merchant Banking and Shipping Company in Glasgow – I promise you, as good as the richest man in Scotland. You have turned up a trump card at last, my dear.'

When she raised this matter with Horace Firth he laughed. 'Oh,' he said, 'my Papa is rich, I agree – But what does that matter? I have no concern for money.'

What he did not explain was that the richest man in Scotland had cut off his son's allowance – further, cut his son out of his will – because of his unrepentant gambling. Horace Firth lived on a small legacy from a grandfather, and such sums as his mother could privily send him. The full explanation Horace did not accord his wife until after their marriage; after which he proceeded to gamble away the pittance they had between them.

And Mrs Firth's younger sisters, Anne and Maria, soon after married gentlemen of adequate means and respectable professions. It was small wonder that when her husband died, Mrs Horace Firth felt humiliated and degraded. She had done nothing to deserve such ill luck; anything her family and friends provided to help her she saw not as charity, but as due recompense. Secretly she grudged her son the support he received from his Uncle George; could not a cheaper school be found, and the difference be granted to his mother whose gowns and bonnets were few and shabby? And now, when she heard of John's scheme of renting a country mansion, disbelieve it as she might, she insisted that John owed her her share in any profitable project of his.

Shivering in his dishevelled Bristol house she kept up her questions and taunts until her brother at least retracted the tale of renting the mansion; he maintained that he had not in the first place said quite that; he was to borrow the mansion, only – indeed, to reside there while he did his friend the great favour of attending to the necessary repairs.

'What do you know of repairing mansions?' demanded Mrs Firth with a glance at the tumbled stone blocks of John's portico. 'Are you to clamber about with hammer and nails—'

16

'No, no. I am to be in charge and to direct the work-men—'

'Then I do not understand why you should not give house-room to your mother and sister.'

'Well, and I cannot be bothered with you, simply.'

'That is evident. But if the house is as large as you imply, we need not be bothered with you, either. – Or do your scruples arise because you are being paid for your foremanship?'

'I am not to be paid,' cried John. 'The arrangement is, that I submit to the lawyers such bills as the work incurs, for materials and so on – and am allowed living expenses, such as I myself incur – which will not cover personal visi-tors—'

'Indeed. Your friend must have great confidence in you.'

'And why not?' shouted John indignantly.

'Well, and I am sure I would not undertake to pay any bills of yours without setting a limit. Have you,' she added in a sharper tone, 'any written authority for this plan, from the absentee landlord?'

'Of course,' John retorted, clapping a hand to his pocket.

'Show me.'

Pouncing after his hand, ignoring his oaths, she drew out a crumpled paper that appeared to be a tailor's bill; on the back of it was scrawled – by an impatient hand and by candlelight:

'I authorise John Thorpe to undertake what improve-ments are necessary at my estate. Frederick Tilney.'

There was a silence. 'Good God,' uttered Mrs Firth at last.

'Are you satisfied? Give me that paper.'

'*That* family? How come you to be in touch with them?'

'How not? I have many acquaintance—'

'But – Frederick . . . Of course, the old General died – So the Abbey is his? And Frederick is your absentee owner?'

John brightened. 'No wonder you are amazed – I had forgotten that you once knew them – and that the young

17

Captain Tilney paid court to you in Bath and threw you over. Well, then,' cutting through Mrs Firth's denials, 'that settles the matter. I hear he does not often visit his Abbey – but there is every likelihood that he will; you will not bear to be there if he does arrive—'

'On the contrary,' said Mrs Firth, deliberately calm and provoking, folding the note, 'after so many years it can make no difference; in fact, it might be quite interesting.'

John clapped his fists to his brow and groaned aloud.

John Thorpe was in some haste to depart for Gloucestershire. He was by now brimming with the enthusiasm and confidence that any fresh plan roused in him; he had acquired several large books on ecclesiastical architecture and was becoming an expert on the subject. Apart from this he was eager to deprive himself of Mrs Firth's company; he said to her:

'You may stay in this house if you will not go back to Anne's. I cannot take you with me and that I swear.'

'Spoken like a dutiful brother. You, too, are casting me out—'

'On the contrary, I am offering you shelter. Or you could go to Maria's; it must be some ages since she last cast you out.'

This appeared to Mrs Firth to be her only immediate recourse. She was not as unaffected as she had pretended by the suggestion that the absentee Frederick Tilney might not in the event turn up at the Abbey; moreover, from what John told her of the state of that venerable pile, it might be as uncomfortable as his house here in Bristol. She wrote to her sister Maria, complaining that John was turning her away and had insulted her, and asking to be met in the market town half way between Bristol and Maria's village. John grudgingly despatched her thither, his manservant driving the mended cabriolet and a new horse; the wheels did not fall off, and the servant's handling of the reins was gentler than his master's; they drew up before the expected time outside the inn; Mrs Firth began:

'I do not suppose there will be anyone to meet me—'

But a merry hail interrupted her. 'Holla, ma'am! I am come to meet you. You made good time; are you well?'

This was her nephew, her sister Maria's eldest son Robert. He was a strong and cheerful youth of seventeen, beaming as if he were delighted to see her. In no time he had hauled her boxes into his trap, ascertained that she would not like to pause for refreshment, offered her some shawls in case she felt cold, and leaping aboard the trap borne her away.

This kind welcome gratified Mrs Firth but, according to her view of life at this juncture, carried an undertone of complaint that directed her thoughts to envy of Maria: Why had not Mrs Firth also a strong willing son to cherish her? Her Roland was older than Robert; why was he never at hand when he was needed? In truth, she was badly used even by those nearest to her. She must bring Roland to some sense of his duty.

It was to Roland that the conversation turned very soon after Mrs Firth's arrival at the commodious parsonage wherein Maria, her mother and husband, and her many children dwelt. Mrs Thorpe had devoted her life and its long widowhood to admiring and indulging her children, and by now was pursuing the same course with her grand-children. Before she made any inquiries of Mrs Firth's health or wellbeing – much less of her misfortunes – she was asking: 'And how is dear Roland? Why could you not have brought him with you? I dare say, he is very busy, studying – does he not take the examinations for his degree this spring? How I wish him success – He has worked so hard, has he not?'

'I expect so. I have not seen or heard from him. What do you know of this absurd plan of John's, to patch up a ruined abbey—'

'Oh my dear, John knows what he is doing – He has so many abilities – But still no children ... Where would we

19

be, without ours? I wonder what Roland will do when he has his degree. I hope, he may take orders; do you not think that would be best?'

Mrs Firth shrugged. 'I had not looked so far ahead. He has no one who could offer him a living – I have no useful friends with influence; he would end up only in some small country parish on three hundred a year, and that would be no help to me.'

Maria's husband, the Reverend Victor Hammond, looked up from his book to say: 'There is little else open to a young man with a classical education in these times; apart from teaching—'

'Upon my word,' exclaimed Mrs Firth, 'that would earn him even less. George would seem to have invested his money to no profit for Roland nor for me.'

Mr Hammond said smiling: 'Let us hope Roland gains some profit other than financial from his uncle's generosity.'

'So he may, but that does not interest me; nor would it you, if you were in my destitute circumstances.'

'But my dear,' cried her mother, 'you are not quite without means – Your father left you what he could – How I wish I could do more for you! You should not be dependent on Roland – the poor boy will want to marry and have children of his own—'

This was to look even further ahead and Mrs Firth was even less interested. When Mrs Thorpe persisted; 'Oh, how I wish too that your dear Horace's father – with all his riches – would be of some help!' Mrs Firth said angrily:

'Horace's father died some years ago with his will unaltered. I choose to have nothing to do with that family. Nor did I come here to be wearied by your nagging about money. Leave me alone!'

Her mother perforce did, which made Mrs Firth feel that no one sympathised with her. Reminded, however, she presently wrote to her son in Oxford:

'My dear Roland: It does not occur to you to write to me

and ask how I do. What I must tell you is that when your term ends you must not go to your Aunt Anne's. Your uncle George has treated me most unkindly and I have quit the house. Loyalty forbids you to have more to do with them. I am at present at Dellingham and your Aunt Maria may have you here. I need your support as any dutiful son would know. It is time you finished with your education and grew to be of some use in the world. Your affec. mother I. M. Firth.'

The days passed, rainy and chill. Mrs Firth hoped that her brother was suffering under the leaking roof of his abbey. She not greatly comforted by her son's reply to her letter:

'My dear Mama: My intentions are dutiful but I deeply regret that they have lately been stretched in many directions; my examinations for my degree take place during this next week; please forgive my preoccupation? I will inform you as soon as I am free of academic obligations (which I hope my dutifulness will reward with a 2nd class?!) and meanwhile must remind you that, as I told you at Christmas, I have promised to go directly from here to Birmingham to resume my duties towards young Charles. His health continues to improve, they tell me, and Mr Ballard hopes he will be able to go to school next half – if he catches up in time with his Greek. The Ballards pay me pretty well and if I have a degree I can demand an increase! £1 per year at least . . . I have nothing to spend money on in that household apart from my washing – I shall be able to send you a little pin-money. I hope you are well, and please give my love to all at Dellingham; has Robert had any luck with the new gun dogs? Harriet embroidered for me such a pretty needlebook – did she tell you? Of course I use needles – for taking splinters of worn-out desk from my fingers. Wish me luck – especially for Monday; if they ask me of Thucydides I *may* reward Uncle George's valued faith in me. (How

21

can you find him unkind?) Your dutiffectionate son, Roland Firth.'

This letter Roland's affectionate mother found in every way offensive. It was frivolous, disrespectful, self-concerned, and implied that he sided with most of the family against his own mother; needlebooks, indeed – 'pin-money' – Mrs Firth had forgotten (if he had told her) that his final examinations were due, and that he had undertaken to spend his summer in such an outlandish place as Birmingham; who was 'young Charles'?

It was apparent that, at this moment, Roland was in no need of a mother's care and guidance, and Mrs Firth resented it. It would serve young Roland right were she to join his Uncle John in Gloucestershire – leaving no address.

3

At the Abbey, until the advent of John Thorpe, everything had been proceeding in a normal and peaceful fashion. The late General had conducted all the affairs of the estate with such military precision and thoroughness that the impetus survived him; even now, five years later, it barely began to slacken. Mr Benson might tire a little of responsibility, and Mrs Wight the housekeeper might deplore the disuse of the main drawing room and of so many bedrooms, but the defects appearing in the fabric were no greater or more frequent than those occurring when the Abbey was a permanent residence; those suggested by John Thorpe were possibilities rather than probabilities; one weed beside the driveway was automatically noticed, and removed, by Mr Benson – who, allowing himself to complain at all to a casual friend of the Colonel's, had no sense of disloyalty or of displaying incapacity. The staff would have liked their master to live here, in order to have their work appreciated; perhaps they were relieved of the tyranny of the 'old General' but they did not behave the worse for that.

'So what is this Mr Thorpe expecting us to do?' Mrs Wight asked the butler. 'And how long will he be here? We shall open the bedrooms in the west gallery, do you think, Mr Brook?'

'That is in your province, Mrs Wight. Downstairs, since he announces he is coming alone, I shall not open the drawing room or dining room; probably he can use the breakfast room, and the Staffordshire service. I hope the weather will be pleasant for him.'

It promised to be; the rain had ceased, and blackbirds sang in the hedges that the gardeners must already start to trim. There was work enough to distract attention from the stranger who walked about watching.

It could not escape John Thorpe's observation that with the improved weather much of winter's damage was swiftly repaired and tidiness restored. Mr Benson in his office filled in pages of his account-book with: '. . . To 2 tons fresh gravel for east driveway . . . To varnish for back staircase and rails . . . To 10 yards chain link fence for north coppice . . .' in his exquisite fine handwriting. John was called upon for no advice, and indeed he enjoyed the interval of strolling about in the sunshine, not so much as reminding himself to look important. He had refused the Colonel's half-hearted offer of payment; he must feel free to assemble his own ideas as they came to him; meanwhile with free lodging and the anticipation of a free hand in improving the estate he was briefly content. Let others – these underlings – replace slates and clear ditches; John Thorpe's contribution was to be more inspired and permanent: He would restore the Abbey to a glory it must have had before the old General's time; he intended to rebuild its chapel.

The butler, Brook, seemed well informed on the subject of the house. 'Yes, sir, I believe there was a chapel – Must have been, when the Abbey was founded. But the family as far as I know has always attended the parish church at the south gate, whose lodge was built at the time of the General's father. The wall of the domain, and the lodges, were built then; the church itself is part Norman—'

'Yes, well, the chapel; surely, it was part of the central layout?' But Brook, whose sense of history dated back only

24

to the time of the General's father, could not locate the site of a chapel. 'I will tell you whom to ask, sir: The Reverend Henry Tilney, the younger son of the General.'

'Yes, well,' said John, impatient, 'if there is no place for a chapel we can place it where we will.' Quoting from his recent reading he said with a wave of his hand: 'It should be of the Perpendicular style, which was the finest style of the later fourteenth century in England, and would correspond with the style of window in the great hall of the Abbey.'

'Yes sir,' answered Brook in a neutral tone. Later in the servants' dining room he repeated Mr Thorpe's words with some mirth, which was shared by his hearers, who were prepared to tolerate their master's eccentric friends, without taking Mr Brook's account at all seriously. 'A Perpendicular chapel,' mused the head footman. 'That would be a marvellous surprise for the Colonel, eh.'

Indeed that was exactly what John Thorpe intended. He had told Mrs Firth that he was doing his friend a favour; his own benevolence warmed him as he warmed increasingly to his project. He would amaze and delight the Colonel; far from repairing the property he would enhance it. He sent for the estate's head stonemason and together they paced the side of the original cloister where the old cells had lain.

'At the top of the garth – Here, where this sunken stone could have been the lowest step of a doorway – This could have been the entrance of the chapel.'

'If you say so sir; could'a bin.'

'And the east window of the chapel must have been on the east side of the building, am I not right?'

'Reckon so, sir.'

John glared at the archway and wall confronting him, trying to render it transparent. 'What is in *here?*'

'Well – It'll be the passage to the offices; the stillroom, I reckon, and the dairy – or mebbe, the lower laundry . . .' The man, stepping under the arch, ran his thumb over a massive block in the wall. 'Aye,' he conceded,' some of these stones, they'm older . . . Mebbe part of your chapel.'

Accepting without comment the appropriation, John Thorpe blew out his cheeks and cried: 'Laundry! Dairy! Desecration! This is intolerable!'

The stonemason reported on this interview to Mr Brook who said: 'Desecration? Perhaps he is a religious man?'

'Wouldn't a thought so, Mr Brook,' said the stonemason.

Mr Brook shook his head, then said in a more alert tone: 'Come, Tom, while I have you, let us go and see what we must tell Mr Benson about the lintels of the side doors,' and off they briskly went, forgetting the chapel.

John Thorpe, absorbed in crawling and stretching with his measuring tape, unable to make his measurements tally, banging his head on protruding stones and forgetting the number he had just calculated, used language that would have confirmed the stonemason's supposition; he had no desire to serve God or the Colonel in his zeal, but rather pictured himself as master architect and builder. Willingly forgetful of all his normal affairs he was the more irritated, next day, to receive a letter from Mrs Firth.

'Hell take her! How can she know this address!' he muttered, about to throw away the letter; then ripping it open he said to himself: 'Well, I suppose, she knew these Tilneys in the old days – How was I fool enough to let her know the name?' Carelessly he scanned the page:

'My dear John: My ill luck pursues me. I hope you are still at your friend's Abbey since I have again been let down by those whom I trust. My only child has gone without consulting me to some people in Birmingham I never heard of. He says he now has a degree which he takes to mean he need no longer have to do with his family. Mama goes to take the waters at Leamington and has not invited me to accompany her. I think she is not well but needs no waters and it would be better for the both of us to come to you for country air and quiet. If I go to Leamington at my own expense next week she can bring me from there and we shall stay until we are both rested and stronger. Maria says she is busy with her garden but I do not know what she does in it. Let me know where you can come to meet me and Mama on our way as it will be an expensive journey for her. Yr affec. sister I.M. Firth'.

Here was a pickle. John decided he could do nothing about it. At a safe distance from Mrs Firth, and very busy besides, he could afford to let her deal with her own troubles. He had enough filial feeling to regret that his mother was not well, but her other daughters could help her – nor was Mrs Thorpe herself wholly incapable of decision. Were his sister put to the charge of her own transport from Dellingham to Gloucestershire, John had a suspicion that she would pay if she must. Were she determined to come to the Abbey, her poverty would not prevent her. In any case, John was disposed to blame her for her rift with her late husband's family; forgetting his own part in recommending the marriage, John well remembered how hostile she had been throughout to the elder Firths; it was small wonder that they had not treated their widowed daughter-in-law with any compassion or generosity. Well, let her do as she pleased; John reading over her letter again noted that boring young Roland had his degree; if that freed him from his Mama in any way, good luck to him.

That his mother would inflict herself uninvited upon the Abbey, John doubted. Nor did he intend to invite her – much less to invite his sister; but a lingering childhood caution made him apprehensive that his sister might well appear like a witch on a broomstick, a Carabosse in his chapel; superstition caused him to send for the housekeeper.

'Oh – Mrs Wright—'

'Wight, sir,' the housekeeper gently corrected him. John had represented her to the Colonel as senile and inefficient, but had to admit, now he recollected, that she was nothing of the kind. She kept the housemaids scurrying under her sharp eyes and let no fault – even a master's mistake in her name – pass.

'Well, Mrs Wight, I might – that is, it might happen – that a lady arrives here—'

'Oh, is Miss Paulina to come, then, sir?' The sharp eyes brightened as Mrs Wight clasped her hands together and smiled.

John had never heard of any Miss Paulina and could bear no more interruptions and complications. 'God knows who is coming,' he said, gloomily. 'But I cannot be troubled about it.' He strode off, his measuring tape unwinding in his wake.

Probably it was as well that John Thorpe did not deny, to the quick-witted Mrs Wight, any knowledge of Miss Paulina. In the first place he had seen the young lady often enough, if he did not remember her name; and in the second place, she was the elder daughter of his supposed great friend, Frederick Colonel Tilney; and she was a great favourite at the Abbey.

Colonel and Mrs Tilney were not too fond of the company of children and it had been their practice, in the days of the 'old General', to send their little girls with their nurse or governess to spend several weeks of each summer at the Abbey; often, they would go on thence to spend more time with their uncle the Reverend Henry Tilney at the parsonage of Woodston. Paulina, the elder, loved the Abbey, the countryside and the company of her little cousins at Woodston; her younger sister Annabella from an early age preferred the pleasures of town, longed only to be old enough for balls and a life of fashion and was, it was possible, more terrified than Paulina of their fierce grandfather. However this was, at the death of the old tyrant Annabella exclaimed: 'Oh, now we need not go to the Abbey – We may go to Brighton with Mama!' while Paulina cried: 'Oh no – I could not bear that! I *must* see everyone at Woodston – and the Abbey!'

By this summer of John Thorpe's irruption on the scene, the pattern had been established, that Annabella spent her time in attending her parents or friends at fashionable watering-places while Paulina passed hers at Woodston – and at the Abbey. Her uncle Henry would drive her over, pause to greet his old friends among the remaining servants and then, for as much as four weeks, Paulina was mistress of the Abbey and all its splendours. She was so highly in favour here that she took her meals with Mrs Wight in the housekeeper's room, took the reins of Mr Benson's gig as he drove about the estate, then put on an apron and helped to churn the butter in the dairy.

Of all this her parents knew nothing; they made the slightest and politest inquiry into their daughters' concerns. Little did Paulina's father suspect that, had he wished to verify the tales told by John Thorpe about the condition of the Abbey, he had a reliable and observant witness at his own dining-table. Nor, need it be added, had Paulina been informed of the presence and intentions of John Thorpe at the Abbey.

The Miss Tilneys were now seventeen and eighteen years old and, as their father had mentioned to John Thorpe, marriageable. John himself had noticed them in Bath and had danced once or twice with either of them without being able to tell them apart; they were both pretty and, he judged, as vain and silly as their mother. John Thorpe's judgements were not infallible, but he was not alone in perceiving Mrs Tilney to be superficial, greedy and brainless, to put it unkindly; her prettiness had faded and she tried to brighten it with paint and jewellery; she was petulant, demanding, and difficult to live with; her husband had been reduced to: 'Yes, my dear' and 'Certainly, my dear' and to escape as soon as possible to the billiards or smoking room. What John Thorpe did not allow for was the docility of both daughters under such an example. Paulina wore what her mother chose in the way of ball gowns, submitted to her mother's hairdresser, and if she danced gracefully, that might not be instantly apparent; Annabella more sincerely did respect her mother's taste, and felt she must live up to it, and was at times conspicuously flirtatious. It was not surprising that Annabella determined to seize a husband at the first opportunity; or that Paulina, this year, longed more than ever to be at the Abbey.

Mrs Wight was more than ever glad to understand that Miss Paulina could be expected, since a few weeks ago Miss Paulina had written to say that there was a plan afoot for her sister and herself to go to France with their parents. 'But I hope,' said Mrs Wight to the eldest housemaid, 'that the plan has fallen through and that we shall soon have her here.'

'What about this Mr Thorpe, though?' asked the maid. 'How can Miss Paulina bear him crawling about and banging the walls – And where shall they take their meals? Must she join him in the breakfast room? It would not be fitting for her to sit with you while that lunatic uses the family rooms?'

'We shall let Miss Paulina decide,' said Mrs Wight comfortably. 'It is her house, and she must tell us what to do.'

Mrs Wight set about preparing the house for Miss Paulina's coming, which involved such extra touches as the tuning of the pianoforte, the airing-out of the finest quilts, and the placing of urns planted with flowers on window ledges. If John Thorpe had observed any of this he might have felt such refinements excessive in his sister's honour; but he had forgotten about his sister and her letter. Nor did the maids, discovering a few inevitable additional defects such as a loose window pane or a new gilt frame needed for one of the ancestral portraits, think of reporting these to Mr Thorpe, who in any case was elusive at present. John Thorpe, finding the Abbey staff of masons equally elusive, had begun to suppose that he must hire staff from the further neighbourhood, and that he would require a quantity of new-quarried stone, whatever the yield from the walls that he would be compelled to demolish. He was not tired of his project but it had tired him, to a point whereat he found it pleasant to ride about countryside in the sunshine, inquiring of quarries or stone carvers, pausing at inns to rest and to boast of his undertaking.

Mrs Wight had a letter from Miss Paulina who was about to leave London for Woodston, whence she would presently come on to the Abbey. Normally she would stay for a few weeks with her uncle Henry; Mrs Wight was in no hurry to advise Mr Thorpe of Miss Paulina's advent, had he been available to hear of it. Meanwhile no one advised anyone of the arrival of the forgotten Mrs Firth, who despairing of her brother's help, mounted her broomstick and appeared unannounced at the Abbey on a balmy spring evening.

4

The broomstick had, for this last part of Mrs Firth's journey, taken the form of a hired carriage for which she would make her brother pay; a night on the stage coach had exhausted her own purse and spirits. That her brother, upon her arrival, was evidently nowhere to be found, was not allowed to trouble her; the staff of the Abbey was not easily thrown into consternation. Mrs Firth was received courteously and conducted to the breakfast room, while Mr Brook paid the coachman from the household coffer, and Mrs Wight sent housemaids scuttling up to prepare a bedroom and the kitchen prepared broth and cold meats. A footman was posted to watch for Mr Thorpe who, strolling through from the stable yard twirling his whip, whistling to himself in the twilight and admiring the swifts that skimmed about the chimney pots, was confronted by the footman bowing and gravely proclaiming:

'Mrs Firth is here, sir.'

'The devil. – Where?' Being told, John Thorpe glanced from side to side as if for escape, but the man held open for him the door into the front of the house; shrugging, John strolled on to greet his sister with:

'Why are *you* here?'

'I will tell you.' Mrs Firth was almost too tired to draw breath, or to eat; she had sipped at some wine, and thrown off her widow's veil which, as protection against dust, she had worn for travelling, little as she felt the veil suited her.

'I am sure you will. The usual sorry yarn. But you could have warned me.'

'I did. I wrote to you. You will pretend you did not receive the letter.'

Ignoring that, John scowled at her and asked: 'What did you tell the servants – How did they look; did you explain—'

'I said I was your sister, that is all,' said Mrs Firth yawning.

'Did they believe you?'

She gave him a cold glance. 'If that is the sort of reputation that has followed you into deepest Gloucestershire, I am sorry for you.'

'Well, and if you want to settle yourself upon us here, I am sorry for *you*.' Pulling out a chair he sat to the table; his books and plans had been tidied away – out of order, he was sure – on to a sideboard, and a cloth laid. Just then a footman entered with a tray, from which he laid out plates and dishes. When he had left, Mrs Firth looking about asked:

'Is this the dining room? It is small, for such a place.'

'No, no. You should see the dining room. It is as large as a cathedral. They do not use it—'

'I forgot; you are only a minion here.' The fragrance of the broth had roused Mrs Firth a little. She lifted her bowl wearily. Broth had been brought for John Thorpe too, but he had lost his appetite – having anyway dined at an inn. He slapped his riding whip against his boot and declared:

'I am not a minion, by G—. Do not try to provoke me. I am engaged in a major work here: I have been asked to rebuild the chapel of the Abbey.'

By now, he had come to believe this. If Mrs Firth did not, she was willing to let it pass for the present. 'Then I imagine you expect to be here for some time. Good.'

'But I do not expect *you* to be here—'

'I have nowhere else, and besides I am much concerned about Roland—'

'Spare me, my dear.'

'Oh, I will spare you – I shall not trouble you in your great work. But I must stay until my nerves are restored.'

'But if Colonel Tilney and his family come—'

'In a house with rooms of *cathedral* size,' returned his sister, 'I can hardly be in anyone's way. Now I *must* retire. Not that I shall sleep; my headache is so fierce that I shall not be able to close my eyes.' Her eyes were already more than half closed as, with the manner of one at a wayside inn, she summoned a servant to conduct her to a room. Nor, flinging herself into a bed, did she stir until woken by a shaft of sunlight that crept into the room at daybreak.

How careless of the servant, she thought, not to close the curtains fully. But, as she rose and went to the window, she was soothed in spite of herself by the beauty of the morning. Birds sang, a soft breeze stirred, and long shadows blue with dew lay across lawns and blossoming trees. Before she could recollect the troubles of yesterday, her nerves responded to the natural calm. 'How peaceful it is,' she said to herself. 'I could almost feel myself at home here.'

Being at home, Mrs Firth felt free to exercise her curiosity about her surroundings. Dressing quickly she left the room and passed along a gallery that led to the magnificent oak stairway; from its window she studied the central quadrangle of the buildings, reminded that this had been an abbey; she opened the door of a room similar to hers, but with a larger window, and hangings prettier and more elaborate; she wondered why this room should not have been allotted to herself? There seemed to be no one about; taking a back stair at the foot of the gallery, she found her way through an anteroom into the main hall, and thence, tempted by the sunlight, out to the gravel sweep and the dappled shade of a shrubbery walk. To find herself awake before others – and out of doors so early, and alone – gave her a sense of satisfaction that would have bloomed into wellbeing, had it not brought with it the memory of her unfortunate circumstances. Even these, however, could not weigh upon her too painfully as the scent of daphne and syringa wafted in the warming air.

'How well I should be,' Mrs Firth thought, 'if I were to live in the country in a place as pleasant as this. How I should retain my youth and my looks . . .' She could fittingly have employed the word 'regain' of her youth, since she had a son of twenty years old, but she was slow to relinquish the hopes and ambitions of her own youth; indeed her life had given her nothing more than the daydreams of a ballroom belle to look forward to. Some uneasy association in her ideas made her add to herself: 'And how well Roland would be, after some weeks here.'

Roland was not unwell – yet, but his mother had lately suffered unusual maternal solicitude. Angry as she was that her son had defiantly taken himself off to Birmingham, she had been disturbed by the tone of his letter, written thence to Dellingham. Roland had apologised for his adherence to his own promises, and explained that they had indeed been promises, and that he felt himself useful and necessary in the Ballard household. 'Poor Charles,' Roland wrote,' 'has not been able to do much studying as he has been confined to bed with what the doctors say is a low kind of typhoid fever. He brightened considerably when I arrived and I hope we shall soon be at our books; his fear of missing school does not improve his health and as it is, they do not now think he will be fit until after Christmas. Between us, dear Mama, I could wish that my worthy employer Mr Ballard were a little less successful in his business! He is saving his gains for the purchase of a country estate, but in fact, his business is his life – and he must meanwhile live near it, and in a proximity that cannot do his precious son any good. The house, well appointed as it is, is situated in a hollow, and in the miasma and fumes from the steel foundry;

also he has a railway line building, and the canal is extended
– and floating with coal dust and burgeoning with fatal-
looking insects; if the summer is hot – and the weather here
is already stuffy and humid – and I am not at all happy
about the drains ... Forgive me, this is not a topic for a
lady's ears – or in this instance, eyes. I mean only to mention
that I am for the present the more committed to my eager
pupil. Did I tell you that Uncle George sent me a guinea
on hearing that I had my degree? When I can go into the
city I shall buy perhaps a new lexicon, to encourage Charles.
His father has given him a puppy, a boisterous little spaniel,
to cheer him; the beast is as yet rather too boisterous for
his nervous master so he sleeps on my bed – The puppy, I
mean, of course. I hope soon to teach him to obey me in
the cause of peace (again, I refer to the puppy).'

The implications of this letter did not at all please Rol-
and's affectionate mother. An unhealthy air – bad drains –
a dog on the bed ... Why should only the spoilt young
Charles suffer? Why should books be bought for a boy who
already had all he desired? Why should Roland at peril to
his own health remain in such surroundings? As she turned
back towards the Abbey on this exquisite morning Mrs Firth
resolved:

'How well Roland too would be, if he were to come here.
I shall not allow him to sacrifice himself; he is too obliging;
that boy could find another tutor – in any case he will never
be fit for school, as he goes on. I shall write to Roland and
bid him come to the Abbey. He is my only child and I have
seen almost nothing of him for years. He can have one of
those dozens of bedrooms I saw, and he will be no trouble.
I shall write at once.'

As she followed a flagged path that emerged from the
end of the shrubbery she heard hooves, and saw her brother
John on a stout bay cob, trotting off along a driveway to a
lodge gate; Mrs Firth was convinced that John had pretended not to see her. She did not try to detain him, but as

she watched him go she reflected: Roland will be no trouble
– but let us hope John is not up to any caper that will bring
us all to confusion.

This notion, clouding a little the brilliance of the morning, sent her indoors in search of breakfast before she
sought some paper and pen for the writing of her letter;
she must do that before John could prevent her.

While she awaited a reply from Roland she explored the
Abbey and its grounds, at a leisure which wrought an
improvement on her nerves and restored her to some sense
of her own dignity. She wondered that she had been in what
now appeared to have been a panic flight about the country,
from one unwelcoming refuge to another – and wearing
her widow's veil as if that might protect her; she was now,
she recognised, in a setting more fitting, and to which her
birth and beauty entitled her. She should be the mistress of
a demesne as expansive and gracious as this.

She came to observe that the Abbey, absent as its owner
might be, was well tended; the servants were neat and busy
and their manners obliging; it too had dignity. How far this
was owing to the lingering spirit of the old General she
could not know, but it pleased her. The prevailing tidiness
was marred only by her brother John, whom she rarely
saw, but whose books and papers were scattered about the
breakfast room and whose boots and hats she saw being
gathered up from passages and hallways by the obliging
servants. One morning she found him in a corner of the
cloister, striking with a hammer at small blocks of stone and
strewing the pavement with scraps of rubble.

'What *are* you doing?' she inquired in a forbidding tone.

John Thorpe had recently learnt that bedded rock, such
as limestone, must be hewn with its grain rather than against
it, in order to render the surface weather-resistant. He was
trying to ascertain for himself the distinction and was not
glad to be interrupted. Smiting with his hammer so sharply

that a chip of stone skimmed in the direction of his sister's face he answered briefly:

'Go away.'

Mrs Firth, naturally, did not; she chose this opportunity of telling him that his nephew was summoned to the Abbey.

'Is he, by G—. And who invited him?'

'I did, of course. What could be more natural?'

That question did not detain John; he growled: 'Well, and who invited you, for that matter?'

Mrs Firth, also undetained, remarked: 'If you remember, I intended at first to bring Mama. I cannot see that this is any different.'

This piece of feminine illogic made John throw down his hammer and run his hands through his hair, showering himself with stone dust. 'You will be behaving soon as if you owned the place. Will you leave me *alone* . . .'

Dreaming that she did in fact own the place Mrs Firth drifted away, pausing to watch a gardener who was tying up a climbing rose, already in bud, beside an arched doorway. 'I,' she decided, 'would have more roses – For all the length of that wall, I would set them.'

When she heard from Roland that he was persistently determined to share with poor Charles the pestiferous summer vapours of Birmingham, she was as amazed as indignant.

'How dare he!' she exclaimed. 'This is outrageous!' But she was as determined as was Roland, and soon she thought of a solution from the *impasse*:

'Well then, all I can say is, that if he cannot be separated from the tiresome child, he must come and bring the creature *with* him!' And forthwith she sent a footman to bring paper and pen.

5

Jacob Ballard was devoted to his life's work to the point of dedication. He had a vision of a new age – for his country, nay for all mankind – wherein travel, commerce, civilisation – life itself – would be made easy by the inventions of this modern industrialised society; there would be railways up and down the entire country, bringing people into closer touch and hence into harmony; the mills and manufactories would pour forth their bounty, produced in vast quantity by the simple use of machines, and available to all; the possibilities were enormous. At times he hardly dared look ahead, so great was the prospect; but meanwhile, he was too much engrossed in the labours of the moment to speculate on their results. What he could himself achieve, was his practical aim. A development that gratified him – such as the construction of a railway to bring coal from the coalfields to his steelworks – led on so fast to the next project that he did not pause to congratulate himself. He saw himself as a pioneer of progress; this was a compulsion that he must serve, at whatever risk; there must be some failure and some suffering – but what was ever accomplished without that? He was not personally ambitious nor anxious for gain; his project of setting himself up as a gentleman in a country estate was entertained only to please his wife.

Jacob Ballard was, in short, a man of great energy, toughness and resolution, and he required these qualities in his workers and associates. It may have caused some surprise to those who encountered him in the course of his work, that he was devoted too to his one delicate child, a son.

It was possible, the very perceptive might have supposed, that Jacob Ballard valued in his son the qualities that he himself did not possess. Jacob as a boy had established his power over others with his fists; the acquisition of a farthing had meant riches; he had had barely any schooling; nothing had forced him to yield or cry. Deep in his heart (for he was never able to show his softer feelings) he may have had a special tenderness for this son of his, who was delicate from birth, shy, and clever.

Charles Ballard as an infant had been slow to develop, and when he was two years old he had suffered a form of seizure from which he did not – and some doctors said, would not – recover. He was now over fourteen years old, but looked like a fragile child of ten or eleven; he could not properly use his left arm or hand, and his left foot dragged; the left side of his face was partly numb, which caused his speech to slur, when he felt ill at ease especially. Every known type of treatment had been tried on him, and every doctor had been subjected to his father's powerful anger and scorn. Charles himself had been used to his father's rumpling his hair and shouting: 'Now, young misery, what are we to do with you next? I declare, we shall send you back as fault-in-manufacture and I shall get me a new son!' Yet, oddly, Charles loved his father; the bond between them may have been reversible.

What Charles loved best, as he grew older, was reading; he learnt not only willingly but hungrily. His father entering the schoolroom would cry: 'Books, books, books! I never read a *book* when I was your age!' And Charles's large clear eyes would lift in a half-smile that made his father cuff the boy's head and insist in a bellow: '—And I am none the worse for that!' Whereat Charles would smile more broadly.

'I wonder he is not afraid of you,' Charles's mother would protest.

'He? He is afraid of nothing!' Mr Ballard would affirm – a strange statement, of one so apparently slight and timid.

Charles had a succession of governesses and tutors, some of whose attentions seemed to drive him into illness; his mother suspected that Charles was sometimes lazy; the truth rather was, that he fell ill when he was bored.

'Sir, I do not know why it is,' Charles said to a tutor when he was thirteen years old, 'but I am happy only when I am living in history – or other languages.' He stroked the cover of his French grammar as if it were the head of a dog. This tutor, a student, had come for a summer vacation, and he was the first person to whom Charles had been able to make such a confession. 'I like Latin best. You see, it feels as if I were – It is hard to explain – living in a special world where I can meet people who are dead – but that does not matter . . . We are alive together—'

'Greek is better,' said the tutor. 'Or at least I think so. You will soon see for yourself.' He took a pen and began to write out the Greek alphabet.

That was what drew Charles to this tutor: The tutor did not pause to discuss Charles's notions, but hurried him on; he never asked whether Charles felt tired, or let a piece of poor work pass. 'Use the other hand,' he would say if Charles fumbled in turning a page with his left; he would say it not helpfully, as others might, but impatiently. Charles felt himself, for the first time, running to keep pace.

It was what he had needed. To his parents, when they asked, he said: '. . . No, Mr Firth is not being kind to me; he is sometimes horrid.'

'But, my dear—' began his mother, anxiously.

His father said: 'You have met your match at last, have you?'

As Roland had noticed, Charles made a rapid recovery from his fever when his Greek lessons were resumed. Nevertheless Roland, happy enough about his own health, was not reassured about his pupil's; he would not desert Charles, but at Mrs Firth's invitation for both of them to go to Gloucestershire he was attracted. It was worth consulting his employers; with an intuition that made him aware of the hidden feeling between father and son, Roland raised the matter when Mr Ballard had burst in for one of his visits to the schoolroom.

'Phew,' groaned Mr Ballard pulling up a chair, 'it is stifling in here.' So it was, everywhere, on this day; Roland had chosen to open the windows even to the muffled clanging of the foundry outside. That Mr Ballard had, even for a moment, seated himself encouraged Roland – and so did what he took to be his mother's unusual tact: Scalding as were her reproaches in her letter to himself, she had enclosed a note to 'Mr & Mrs Bollard' – which, misnamed as it was, must be more persuasive than Roland's.

Roland gave the letter to Mr Ballard, who said: 'What is this? Who writes to me and cannot spell?' before reading the letter aloud. Roland, listening, was puzzled and slightly at a loss; how could he account for his mother's writing as if she were inviting his pupil and him to 'her' country estate? The same impression was made upon Mr Ballard, who merely said: 'So your mother owns this Abbey, does she?'

'No, sir,' said Roland, without qualification.

'H'm. She invites you to take Charles there . . . Extensive grounds . . . well-trained staff . . . Have you told Charles of this?'

'No, sir. I thought it best to consult you—'

'Well, the lad is capable of making up his own mind. Boy, do you want to go to Firth's mother's country retreat? Do you think you would like it? You want to go?'

'Very much, sir, if you please,' said Charles, at his most shy. Roland could tell from the faint blush on Charles's cheeks that he was, for his father's sake, understating his preference; and Mr Ballard eyed his son closely before saying:

'Very well then. If you do not like it we will soon send for you. Whom do I write to? She wants to be paid, does she, this mother of yours, for her hospitality?'

'No, sir,' denied Roland with a faint qualm.

'Well then – Write to her yourself. I will tell Mrs Ballard. Mind and leave all your books at home, you poor weakling,' he added to Charles, tweaking at the boy's hair.

Later Charles told Roland: 'He means me to take my books, of course. But my mother says we must take Nurse – How can we avoid that?'

It might have been wise; but Charles was so bright and confident that Roland felt confident too that he could look after Charles well enough himself.

Charles made an unfortunate first impression on Mrs Firth, by arriving at the Abbey in the Ballard carriage, an impressive conveyance itself, with postilions; nor was it to remain here for the use of Master Charles, but to return directly to Birmingham. The immediate reason for this, into which Roland did not enter, was that Nurse had been left behind at the inn of the party's overnight stay, and would be collected on the way back. Nurse, who had been despatched by the pleas of Mrs Ballard, was satisfied that Charles was fit to travel and would assure her mistress of it; she warned Roland only that Charles might be in danger of over-excitement and should take his bromide at bedtimes.

Charles had never before been away from home, except to undergo cures at various fashionable and busy medical centres. Excited he was by the novelty of this excursion and by the pleasure he at once felt on seeing the Abbey; but he was also tired, and his shyness under Mrs Firth's scrutiny rendered his left arm inert and his lips stiff.

'Roland, should you not cut his meat for him?' Mrs Firth

demanded at dinner. Roland, to indicate that Charles need not be spoken across and for as if he were a deaf-mute, asked Charles: 'Would you like me to, Charles?'

Charles knew quite well what impulse of sympathy urged Roland to ask; but in his own need to reply gratefully he could say only: 'Ah . . . ah . . . No . . . N-n-n . . .' He contrived to cut the meat, clumsily since his left hand was not as good an ally as usual; when he laid down the knife and took a fork in his right hand, Mrs Firth raised her eyes to the ceiling and murmured something about: '. . . Table manners . . .'

He was glad of bed time. A housemaid came to show him to his room. 'Wait – I will come up with you,' said Roland, 'and see that you are comfortable—'

'My dear Roland, does the child have to be put to bed? You should have brought his nurse; this should be no part of your duties. – Are you nervous?' she asked Charles, who looked at her in inquiry, shaking his head; as Roland pointedly did not help, Charles managed to say: 'Of . . . of . . .?'

'Oh, well you see, this is an old house, and it was an abbey, if you understand what that means. Ignorant or superstitious people might expect it to be haunted.'

Charles, unmistakably, laughed; that is, the half of a broad smile rippled over his face and his eyes sparkled. Roland, also laughing, followed him and the maid upstairs; he by no means knew the layout of this complicated building yet. He would have apologised for his mother, had that been permissible; as it was he saw Charles to his door and left him to the maid, who was arranging the bed curtains and fussing about in a manner that Charles must see as friendly. Descending the great staircase – was this the way he had just now ascended? – Roland could imagine that confusion might lead to alarm here; at the foot of the stair, when a figure came hurtling out of a door that Roland had not identified in the panelling, he stopped with a shock. The figure – carrying a large axe, wearing a dark cloak – a ghostly headsman? – collided solidly into Roland and swore. Roland said tentatively:

'Uncle John? Good evening—'

'Who the d— are you ?' John Thorpe was cross and exhausted after his experiment in trimming a beam of seasoned sixteenth century oak; he was not perceptibly delighted to be told that this was his nephew Roland. 'So you are come?' he conceded, and strode on across the hallway. Roland, after a false attempt, found the room wherein he had left his mother, and joined her.

'Mama, please be patient with Charles; he is a very clever boy, you know, but you . . . disconcerted him, a little, did you not?'

'Not as much as he disconcerted *me*. Is that the kind of half-wit you spend your time on? Sit down and listen to me. It is time you took your life seriously. Now I have at last gained your presence if not your attention – We must discuss your future.'

Roland, sitting as bidden, regarded her attentively.

'Well,' she went on, 'what have you to say?'

'About my future? I would like to take orders, finally.'

'Finally to what? You cannot depend on your family for ever – you must earn money, do you not see that? You cannot stay in a plague-ridden city attending a moron—'

'Mama, *please*—'

'I am sure you are not paid enough, for such easy work; you must bear in mind that you owe much to your Uncle George – and, after all I have done for you, bringing you up – have I not some claim on you?'

'Yes, you have,' agreed Roland readily. As a thought occurred to him: 'To whom, I wonder, am I to be indebted for my lodging here – mine, and Charles's? To Uncle John?'

'John!' echoed Mrs Firth in sharp contempt. 'He has not even paid for the carriage in which I came here – the butler admits it. It was paid out of the household money—'

'Then I shall repay it,' Roland said. 'I can surely do so,

out of the easy money I have earned at Mr Ballard's. – Who, by the way, offered to pay for my keep and for Charles's, should you require it.'

'God forbid,' exclaimed Mrs Firth, rising, 'that I should ever *require* to accept charity. You insult me. You disappoint me. How have I deserved it, that before you have been two hours in the house you show yourself obstinate and foolish. I wish you had not come.'

Roland did not share that sentiment; he was looking forward to tomorrow, to seeing the Abbey and grounds and to reading the *Odyssey* with Charles. He was sorry that his mother was angry but could not in honesty understand what he had done to offend her. If he himself was not disappointed in his mother he could not in charity admit to himself why not.

6

On the next morning, even before Roland had reimbursed the household for his mother's travel expenses – and had seen Mr Brook delete the item from the pantry ledger – the household had concurred in the opinion that these two guests were more to be welcomed than the previous arrivals. These two were more polite and grateful and moreover Charles established himself at once by reason of his infirmity. 'Why, the poor lad is a cripple!' was enough to generate a natural kindness; that the boy made so little of his own affliction won him admiration.

Mrs Wight was stricken with compunction that she had – justifiably apprehensive of the number of Mr Thorpe's relatives who might yet appear – prepared for Mr Firth and Mr Ballard rooms in the eastern wing of the house, not to be ranked as the best; very pleasant they were, not inferior in furnishings, but they were served by a narrow and steep staircase that led into a passage behind the billiard room. 'And those stairs will be difficult for him – Will he take offence if I offer him another room – What do you say, Mr Brook?'

'On the other hand,' pronounced Mr Brook after pondering, 'that staircase has a strong railing that he can hold to. I imagine that will be safer for him than to use the main stairs where the balustrade is too wide to take a grasp of.'

So Charles, relaxed and refreshed by a night of sleep, descended with the support of the handrail, so blithely that his lameness was hardly apparent. He and his tutor expressed their entire satisfaction with their quarters and with the muffins and eggs of their country breakfast.

'And now he is at his lessons,' reported the footman; he had been about to add: '–poor boy', but no one could have looked more contented than Charles as he sat in the sun of the cloister with a Greek text in hand. 'We should take a table out for them, to lay out their books,' went on the footman, still spying from the pantry window. 'They have chosen a good spot for their studies.'

Mr Brook looking over his colleague's shoulder said: 'Ay, they are sheltered and quiet in that corner – Until such time as our architect begins to knock down the walls and shower them with boulders.'

John Thorpe had made it known that some demolition was imminent; he would not admit that this was beyond his powers but was at present engaged in seeking the outline of the original chapel and tracing its foundations. He must know where to start his excavations; since the chapel had been totally destroyed when the more modern side of the quadrangle was built, and the buildings here did not tally at all with the shape of the chapel, he was still confused, and had to consult Mr Brook, who summoned Mrs Wight to the conference. Any unoccupied household staff peeped round doorways, deeply interested and amazed.

'*This* wall,' said John Thorpe, kicking it, 'I can tell is not thick. What is this room beyond it? Only a part of the offices – what is it used for?'

'We call it the fine laundry, sir;' Mrs Wight explained.

'But you just told me that the vast room over *there* is the laundry.'

'Yes, sir, the main laundry. But this is for muslins and lace – It is needed when the ladies of the family are here, but such fine fabrics as the girls and I wear, can be included in the household wash.'

This economical practice did not seem to John Thorpe to be necessary. 'We can take down this wall then, to make space.' He proceeded, followed by his fascinated audience, out of doors and across a drying green, to bang his fist on a further door in the wall: 'And what is *this*?'

Mr Brook took up: 'That is the servants' boot room, sir.'

John Thorpe blew out his lips; why did servants need boots? Rounding a tall hedge he glanced at his sketched plan and said: 'But here should be the windows of the library.'

'No, sir – This is the room where the grooms keep their capes and hats. There is another door, into the stable yard—'

'I never knew such a hotch-potch of a place . . . Well, do not you all hang about; I can manage; have you no work to do?' The followers melted away. Charles Ballard, drawn to the gathering while his tutor happened to be writing letters, started to melt too, but he could not resist asking Mrs Wight:

'Can you tell me, ma'am, what the gentleman is doing?'

'He means to build a chapel,' Mrs Wight explained.

'What a splendid idea!' Charles cried.

'I am glad,' muttered John Thorpe overhearing. 'Well, that is all I need you for, Brook. Go away, all of you.' Charles did not understand why Mr Brook, as they departed, winked at him.

Charles hurried to Roland to tell him: 'Your uncle is to build a chapel here!'

'My uncle,' replied Roland drily, 'is a man of many enterprises. Come, if you find that so thrilling, you can add a paragraph to the letter to your mother, and tell her of it. Letters to mothers,' he added instructively, 'are very often valued according to their length, and this of yours is brief.' Charles, penitent, obeyed; he did not want his mother to

feel that he was too happy to write to her, though the
distractions of the Abbey absorbed him; he was so well here,
that he was unaware even of feeling well. 'I might have
brought Xerxes here,' he said as he wrote. 'There is so
much ground for him to run in.' Xerxes was his little spaniel;
Charles could have run as fast as he.

During these days, Mrs Firth was less happy than she had
been. The 'bliss of solitude' began to pall; country air and
peace had restored her looks and vitality, but there was no
one to notice that – indeed, to notice her at all. Her brother
John's attention she did not covet; but she thought it per-
verse of her son Roland to ignore his mother in favour of
that hobbling lisping boy he had brought with him. At this
time of year, in the country, there should be society – picnics,
dancing or card parties in the long evenings; it almost persuaded her to write to Colonel and Mrs Tilney, warning
them of the depredations with which John Thorpe
threatened their Abbey; should the Tilneys come, there
would be a change of company. But then it occurred to her
that John Thorpe and his entourage would probably be
ejected from the Abbey; no, that was not what she desired;
absurd as John's activities were, they provided the only pre-
text for his – and his sister's – sojourn here. So, sighing, she
walked about the gardens and the grounds and mourned
the waste of her life – so far.

One morning she sat to rest on a stone bench under
some gently rustling trees on a little knoll that overlooked
the boundary of the parklands. Beyond the wall she could
see a cornfield, starred with poppies among the green
blades, vivid against the darkening green of the woods across
the vale. The landscape was familiar to her by now; what it
required was some human interest, but even the cattle were
grazing elsewhere. Then she perceived two figures, walking
slowly along the verge of the poppy field, as if in conversation. They paused at the field corner, looking right and

50

left, and presently appeared again at the wooden bridge that
crossed the stream below Mrs Firth's knoll, having evidently
entered the park by a gate just out of her sight. Strolling,
they ascended the slope alongside a hedge, still gazing about
them. Mrs Firth rose and made her way along the path that
encircled her knoll, to intercept them; they either had lost
their way or were treating the grounds as their own. She
waited until they were about to step on to the path before
she spoke:

'Good morning to you. I suppose you know that this is
private land?'

The interlopers both looked up, surprised. One was a
young girl in a cotton bonnet and a light summer gown
with scarlet sash; her companion was a tall man in dark
clerical dress.

'Thank you – Yes, we know. I am Paulina Tilney.'

'Oh; yes,' Mrs Firth allowed. 'The housekeeper has mentioned you.'

The gentleman had removed his hat; he said: 'I hope we
did not alarm you in any way by what seemed an intrusion.'

Mrs Firth denied this, with a shake of her head. The
young woman was saying in a cheerful manner: 'My uncle
has brought me from Woodston, but we left the groom to
drive from the lower road because we wanted to walk up by
the fields. It is such a pleasant day, is it not?'

If they wished Mrs Firth to introduce herself they did
not make it evident; nor did they hurry to walk on. It had
taken Mrs Firth some moments to appreciate that here, in
whatever guise, was her change of company. Now she studied
the newcomers with attention. The girl was slender and
carried herself well; she was probably still young enough to
dress in the style of a milkmaid – and, Mrs Firth had
to admit, the simplicity suited her; she had an open and
pleasant countenance. The gentleman was perhaps not as
old as he had at first seemed; there was a melancholy in his
expression that made him solemn rather than elderly –

51

though his hair had streaks of grey, as had the neatly trimmed beard that he wore. He had altogether an air of thoughtfulness – verging on the venerable – that interested Mrs Firth.

She averted her gaze, in order to give him the opportunity of studying herself in turn; he had, she felt, displayed some interest. To the girl she said: 'You will be with us for some little time, then?'

'That is not decided, but I hope so.'

'We seem at present to be a household of menfolk,' Mrs Firth told her, smiling, 'since I have my brother and my son here. So it may be as well that I am with you, to act as chaperone!'

This was acknowledged by a slight bow. 'We shall meet again, then,' said the girl; she took the arm of her companion, to walk on. With a slight bow in turn to Mrs Firth, he moved away. Mrs Firth listened to hear what they said of this meeting, but they did not speak; Mrs Firth, not wishing them to know that her interest in them lingered, set off in another direction back towards the Abbey.

She must soon dress for dinner, and this she did with unusual care. Between wishing to appear elegant to the gentleman, and not wishing to appear so much better-dressed as to put the girl out of countenance, and in any event with so small a choice of garments, deploring as ever her poverty, she finally wore her dark poplin, with no jewellery, but a shawl of delicate lace; she arranged her hair simply – as indeed one must, with no maid; she must find out whether any housemaid here would be of any use as lady's-maid. Fairly well satisfied with the effect, she descended to find the breakfast room empty except for the jumble of her brother's books, notebooks, lumps of stone and muddy boots.

'Mrs Firth,' said a footman who was apparently in wait for her, 'if you please, dinner is served in the west parlour.' He ushered her across the hall, into a room she had not yet

entered but which she had seen to be larger than the breakfast room yet not so vast as the cathedral-sized dining room.
Here she saw Roland, Charles, and the two newcomers. The
table was, as she quickly noticed, laid with a different style
of china and napery; there were flowers in silver vases; and
the young lady, greeting her, was no milkmaid; plain her
gown was, but of the finest material, and she had dressed
her hair with a strand of pearls. Where did the chit imagine
she was – in Bath? What was more, she spoke to Mrs Firth
with all the manner of a hostess:

'Mrs Firth, will you please to take the chair opposite to
mine? And Mr Firth, beside me? We decided,' she went on
to Roland's mother, 'to leave the breakfast room entirely at
the disposal of Mr Thorpe, and to use this room – it has the
evening sun, but if you take this place, it will not catch your
eyes. There are so few of us that it is not worth using the
dining room – which besides, is so much more formal.'

They took their seats. A place had been set – Mrs Firth
presumed, for John – which was not occupied. The clerical
gentleman pronounced the grace and footmen advanced to
serve the dinner. This, at any rate, was no more elaborate
than had hitherto been provided in the breakfast room; but
Mrs Firth felt it would choke her. 'We' decided! John was
to be banished as if he were a common workman! She
maintained an icy silence while conversation began. It was
largely between the boy Charles and the solemn clergyman,
on the topic of the ancient Greeks. The boy, heaven knew
why, stuttered hardly at all; at one point he impertinently
consulted his hostess:

'But, Miss Tilney, surely you had to learn Greek when you
were at school?'

'I wish I had; but I neither went to school nor had much
formal education. Girls rarely do, you know.'

Charles stared. 'Do they not? You see, I have not been to
a school – yet – myself. So what *did* you learn?'

Everyone – excepting Mrs Firth – laughed. Miss Tilney

said: 'I learned to play the pianoforte, and speak French, and to draw sketches of the temples of your ancient Greeks; and to dance.'

'That,' remarked Charles with an innocent satisfaction, 'is more than anyone will try to teach *me*.' No one made any comment; Mrs Firth would have liked to point out that, with his disability, no one would attempt to; but she preserved her silence. From Greek temples the talk moved to other phases of architecture, and presently Miss Tilney addressed Mrs Firth with a directness that could not be avoided:

'Mrs Firth, I am astonished and delighted to know that my father has decided to rebuild the chapel of the Abbey! Is it not a magnificent idea?'

'The idea, I suspect, was my brother's,' replied Mrs Firth in a tone that ascribed blame rather than praise; but Miss Tilney went on as happily:

'Then we must give him all the help we can. It will be a very large undertaking. I believe it will be necessary to do away with some of the newer buildings; my grandfather would be angry! He thought the new offices and kitchens were as admirable as the older parts – but, for myself, I had rather see the entire place as it was originally designed. Is that too romantic?'

'Living in it, as the first occupants did, would certainly not be convenient,' her uncle said. 'One would need to be highly romantic – or hardy – to enjoy it.'

'Well, perhaps all the conveniences will not be swept away in Mr Thorpe's course,' said Roland. 'Indeed, it seems that Mr Thorpe himself is not too sure of some of his plans. Charles has already been called upon to assist him, in correcting a map of the rear premises, and drawing a fresh plan—'

'And how did you come to know better than Mr Thorpe?' Mrs Firth asked Charles, sharply.

'You see, ma'am, one day when he was inspecting the offices, I was watching, and I think he asked me, because . . .'

Because Mr Thorpe was too proud to ask any of the servants, was the half-formed thought in Charles's mind that he felt it incautious to express. In correcting John Thorpe's false placing of the drying green, Charles had himself become interested in the work, but had not dared to express that, either.

'You can draw, can you,' said Mrs Firth in so sceptical a tone that the rest of the company was disconcerted for the moment. Mrs Firth was looking, significantly, at Charles's hands. He had accepted, rashly, a large and slippery pear which he was trying to cut with his silver dessert knife. His limp left hand was needed to steady his plate, but the pear threatened to roll away under the action of his right. Roland was watching; he saw that the footman behind Charles's chair was watching too; and so, he then saw, was Miss Tilney; with a slight movement of her finger she bade the footman forward; the man, silently, stepped to Charles's side and deftly peeled and sliced the intractable fruit. Charles murmured: 'Thank you.'

Roland had already received an excellent first impression of Miss Tilney. This tact and kindness was added to what Charles had been offered by all the staff of the Abbey; one could accept a service from a servant rather than presume to 'help'; had she herself cut the pear – easily within her reach – Roland would have thought the less of her; as it was, he hoped to catch her eye and indicate his approval; but the conversation was resumed, on the subject of the chapel.

'I do not know,' Miss Tilney was saying, 'that there is in existence any picture or plan of the chapel as first built; do you know of one, Uncle?'

'No. But if you remember, there is in the parlour at Woodston an old engraving of the Abbey with the walls of the ruined chapel—'

'Yes, yes; of course. There is not much chapel to be seen, but it must show where it stood?'

55

'I do not know for how long the ruin stood; I believe that in the last century, ruins were even built, and considered to be picturesque—'

'Oh yes; how many picturesque ruins did I not have to copy in my drawing book, and they were easier than Greek temples – one can scribble-in broken stones rather than make straight ones convincing. Perhaps Mr Thorpe would like to see that engraving, however? Shall we send him to Woodston?'

'He might prefer to see it here, for comparison. But it is in that heavy oak frame.—Well,' suggested Miss Tilney's uncle, pushing back his chair, 'might it not be brought here – on a brief loan? It is the least we can do for Mr Thorpe's guidance.'

The conveyance of the heavy picture, and the valuable evidence it might provide, became an issue for the rest of dinner; Mrs Firth's own views began gradually to alter: If the project on the chapel had so much attracted the solemn clergyman, it must indeed be of importance? If he took it so seriously, she must, too. Miss Tilney was a romantic silly girl, but her uncle commanded respect. One had to persuade oneself that the idea was 'magnificent'. Yes, of course, it was. John had all along said so.

The part to be played by John in the magnificence did cause John's sister a moment's anxiety, but meanwhile the question at the table seemed to be: The picture could be fetched tomorrow – Miss Tilney's uncle could go for it – a mere two hours' drive; but who would like to accompany him, to enjoy the countryside?

Miss Tilney, her uncle, and Roland were all smiling at Charles. Mrs Firth was provoked into deciding: That pampered little monster is nothing but a nuisance.

7

It began to appear that the strangely assorted party at the Abbey was becoming united in the cause of the chapel. The engraving from Woodston, lent with the stipulation that it be returned undamaged, was set up in the hallway, and all assembled to study it. John Thorpe's judgement was vindicated in so far as the ruins in the picture extended from the corner of the quadrangle eastwards, to the obliteration of that part of the General's father's modern buildings. One complete arch of the chapel wall remained; it was not, as Roland remarked, of Perpendicular style?

'Oh well, those trees are in the way – Why do these artist fellows have to put such rubbish in?' John Thorpe complained.

'I suppose, the artist wished to make a handsome picture,' Miss Tilney suggested.

'Well, his handsomeness is of no help to me. I shall get young Peg-leg here to make a sketch that leaves out the trees,' John Thorpe announced.

'But sir, what should I draw, in place of the trees?' asked Charles.

'Oh, use your imagination,' urged John Thorpe, with a generous inconsistency.

'He might reasonably leave that faculty to you,' Roland

said. Later, he asked Miss Tilney when they met in the garden:

'Do you not think it might be wise to consult your father, for his advice, before Mr Thorpe does any damage – That is, begins his structural alterations?'

'Yes – Except that my father is in France and I do not know where. I suppose he has given full authority to Mr Thorpe? I confess, I find Mr Thorpe a little . . . impetuous; but yet, we have not seen him, actually, at work; when he is fully engaged in it he may concentrate more. Mr Firth, while I see you, may I mention that he – Mr Thorpe – is very brusque in his manners to your pupil?'

'You should see the manners my pupil puts up with from his own father. I do not think that being hailed as 'Peg-leg' or 'Hoppit' will offend Charles in any way.'

Miss Tilney looked uncertain, but Roland was sure. What neither of these two was sure of, but did not care to admit, was that Roland's mother's manners to Charles were more subtly offensive; Mrs Firth lost no opportunity of making her contempt and irritation with the boy all too obvious. They could neither of them utter any reproach to her; nor would that have had an effect; it might have, had they made her aware that Miss Tilney's uncle also regretted her unkindness to Charles; but of Mrs Firth's designs on that gentleman they had no idea.

'Designs' was, as yet, a strong word for Mrs Firth's purpose; but she had come to wonder, after a few days, how it was that the incumbent of Woodston – having come to the Abbey merely to convey his niece – should remain so long here? She still, from time to time, noticed that he rested his eyes on her when he thought her unaware; it must be more than the scheme of the chapel that held his interest. She was now happier again.

At this moment, her happiness was darkened as she turned a corner of the garden walk to see Roland and Miss Tilney in earnest colloquy and unchaperoned. 'Roland,' she called, 'why are you not at your duties? What is your pupil about? You must not neglect him. You will excuse him, Miss Tilney.'

Miss Tilney went off swinging her basket of flowers, and Roland made his way indoors. This double obedience partly reassured Mrs Firth; she would not have Roland fancying himself in love, or any nonsense of that sort, at his age.

Roland did not fancy himself at best; he knew, seriously, that Miss Tilney was a very lovely young lady, that her manners were altogether charming and that when he caught sight of her his heart seemed to swell a little and that when she spoke to him he felt honoured and delighted; he was almost in awe of her wisdom and gentleness; all this experience was new to him but he did not place it before his duty. He was here to teach Charles and he knew quite well what Charles was now 'about': He was in the breakfast room with John Thorpe, struggling over the reconstruction of the chapel from the engraving; Charles had as bidden drawn a sketch without trees, and was endeavouring to explain his deductions.

'You see, sir,' he said, laying a rule across his paper, 'if you continue the curve as it is shown on this arch, you will make a lancet window; and from the length of the wall, you will fit in three of the same; the chapel must have had three lancet windows – and I mean three on each side; I cannot see why not; so the east end of the chapel must have been . . . here.' He pointed.

'How do you know there were not more windows?'

'Because – do you see where the buttress was placed – and *here* is the corner stone – Let us suppose that the altar was placed . . . here . . . Then it would have stood – by my plan – between the small laundry room and the second stillroom.'

'Would it, begad. Clever little Clodhops . . .'

Roland, listening from the windowseat, was inclined to agree with John Thorpe. Charles seemed to have worked out the scale and proportions of the vanished edifice most plausibly – and who was to say that this exercise might not be as valuable as Greek verbs? John Thorpe, restless after such unusual attention to the speech of someone else, was gathering the papers together and jumping to his feet.

'Right then,' he said. 'I shall show all this scribble of yours to our friend with the beard, and ask him if he agrees. Then we can proceed!'

'Proceed to do what, sir?'

'Why, we shall start digging, and find out whether you are right!'

Something of John Thorpe's enthusiasm infected the others; his bearded friend mentioned: 'Of course, we do not know that this picture was drawn accurately; the legend is, that the whole chapel was destroyed at the Reformation – But if even some foundations remain, it would indicate the size perhaps; not a large chapel, but the community may not have been a large one . . .' He was pacing the outside of the cloister wall, coming up, as John Thorpe had, against a newer wall three feet or so thick. He frowned at it. 'It is so difficult to estimate—'

'By G— it is,' cried John Thorpe. He drew upon himself a reproving glance from his sister who – John could not imagine why – was present at this survey. 'Look here, let us stop this fiddle-faddle and sink a shaft – somewhere – anywhere!'

'What do you expect to find, to prove where the chapel was?' Mrs Firth asked. 'The altar will surely not still be there; nor any pews—'

'There would not, at that time, have been pews,' the reverend gentleman told her. With a wry smile he added: 'At such a time, however, it was often the custom for an abbot who died to be interred behind the altar; would it convince you, Mr Thorpe, if we excavated a coffin or some hallowed human bones?'

'Bones!' screamed Mrs Firth. 'John, you must stop this nonsense at once. It is morbid and reckless.'

'Well, and you need not watch. Go away, do.'

Mrs Firth was ready to. After that threat, she could display a suitable feminine delicacy only by departing; she hoped to be escorted and reassured but the rest of the company was too much engaged in conjecture and measurement, and for the rest of that day she had little company.

In the evening, she settled herself in solitude in the west parlour, where the sunlight was softening towards the rosy hue of sunset and the other members of the party, after dinner, rarely appeared. She had a novel that she longed to read, but it would not accord with the image of herself that she wished now to display. So she had brought her workbox and sat, inattentive to it, gazing out in pensive pose. Rather to her surprise, and to her immediate pleasure, she heard footsteps that passed in the hallway pause, and from the corner of her eye saw her venerable prey look into the room, then approach.

'Mrs Firth; I should apologise for my tasteless remark this morning. I did not intend to alarm you. It is doubtful that human remains would lie in the site of the old chapel – And more than doubtful, at this rate of progress, that Mr Thorpe will discover any.'

'Thank you. Perhaps I am of an unusually sensitive nature; and one is apt to feel – in an old house like this – that hauntings and spectres of the past might occur.' She much enjoyed this occurrence in many of the novels she read – the heroine's candle blowing out, with a skeleton hand reaching from a dark secret passage, and a wailing voice calling her name . . . Her visitor, smiling, came further into the room.

'Any spectre of the past,' he remarked, 'is likely to be only that of the late General. Do you not feel – from what the servants say, and from what my niece tells us – that his displeasure is the threat to our enterprise?'

61

'But the General is dead,' protested Mrs Firth.

'Quite so. But he would much disapprove of the liberties that we might take with his strictly run household – and at times, I suspect some of his staff welcome the chance of defying him – deny that as they would.'

Mrs Firth had no interest in the General or his staff. She said: 'I hope you will remain with us while these ambitious – and perhaps dangerous – schemes proceed. I feel someone of your wisdom and dignity could keep them under control.'

He had drawn nearer, and taken a chair – so placed as it happened by Mrs Firth – opposite to hers. In a tone of faint amusement he replied: 'Yes, I hope to be at hand for the outcome. I did not intend to stay, but I am in no hurry to be elsewhere.'

Mrs Firth, hoping to detain him, had opened her workbox and taken out her netting-needle. Now she looked up in surprise. 'But can you be spared at Woodston? Is someone doing your work there while you are away?'

'I do not work at Woodston,' he said in surprise. 'I have been there on what is in effect a prolonged holiday. My brother-in-law Mr Henry Tilney is the incumbent there.'

'Oh,' said Mrs Firth in bewilderment. She lowered her needle and they stared at each other. He leaned a little forward and said in a serious and gentle tone:

'Do you not feel it is time you and I had a private talk?'

This had come so suddenly that Mrs Firth felt at least that her cheeks had blushed. Her hands began to tremble and the needle fell on to her lap. She could find no words. He went on:

'I do not believe that you have not recognised me.'

'But I – How should – I do not understand . . .'

In the same tone he added: 'I knew you at once, Isabella.'

'You know my name—'

'You knew mine, many years ago. And have you not heard Paulina call me "Uncle James"; or the servants say "Mr Morland"?'

She had not; perhaps Miss Tilney said 'Uncle', or the servants 'sir' – but that was all she had noticed. Now the blush ran hotly over her face and in a hesitant voice she murmured:

'James . . . Morland . . .'

'Yes, you remember now? You truly did not know me?'

Considering that they had at one time been engaged to be married, he might reasonably expect that she would remember him. Mrs Firth admitted this but could summon no excuse for her failure. 'Well – It is no wonder,' she said pettishly. 'It must be your beard. And besides, what should you be doing in a place like this?'

'What indeed; and what should you? I dare say I have changed in many ways. But you have not.'

'No, I suppose I am much as I was,' agreed Mrs Firth, with a hand to a curl of hair. 'And it must be over twenty years – Yet you knew me at once?' She was highly gratified.

'So now we understand each other. I wished to establish that. I had to speak to you in private; I hardly suppose you wish our past association to be known.'

'I cannot see why not,' she said casually. 'In fact I can scarcely remember it.'

'*I* remember,' James Morland said, simply.

He turned in his chair as if to rise, but Mrs Firth was not ready to let him go. 'It was in Bath,' she recollected. 'I was very young. And you were just ordained? You were young, too. Such a marriage might have been unwise?'

He had been, besides young, poor; a living offered to him had been far below what young Isabella hoped for; she had been very unhappy at the time, she did recall – Indeed she thought James had abandoned her; why? A troubling new recollection stirred in her mind . . . But why look back? Mrs Firth lived in the present. There was nothing to be gained by harking back. Mrs Firth saw herself as a totally different person from that girl in Bath – except of course that she had the same beauty. James, if she could still so think of

him, was a different person too. He, however, had improved
– he looked distinguished and was well if soberly dressed;
the air of melancholy that she had observed in him was still
attractive to her. She turned her attention to him.

'And you – are you married?'

'I have not married,' he answered – with a hint of regret?

'I lost my dear husband a long while ago,' she told him
with a hand pressed to her eyes. 'I have had a lonely life—'

'You have a good and faithful son.'

'Yes, Roland . . . But one does need . . . company of one's
own generation; one needs guidance and support.'

'Yet there is much pleasure in the society of young people.
I have many nephews and nieces and am as fond of them, I
think, as I could be of children of my own. For that reason
I am specially glad to be staying for a while at the Abbey; I
shall have the opportunity of seeing more of Paulina than
I have for some time. We meet occasionally in London but,
here, I find her more – if I can put it thus – like her natural
self. She is not happiest in the false world of balls and
gaiety.'

'Nor, I suppose, are you; but for a young girl, there is
nothing wrong with balls!' retorted Mrs Firth, rejecting the
topic of Miss Tilney. 'You live in London, then?' she pursued.

'Yes. I have for a few years held a living in Camden, but
in Advent I am to succeed to a canonry at St Paul's.'

'St Paul's cathedral? Then you have done very well in your
profession!'

'I hope to,' he said gravely.

'And you have a house in London, I suppose?'

'I shall have to move, for convenience, and the house I
have bought requires some repairs.' He added, smiling:
'And so I am passing time in another house that is undergo-
ing the same process—'

'Yes, well, I hardly imagine your London house is on the
same scale as the Abbey.'

'Indeed not; though it is larger than a single man of simple tastes requires.'

He said that, Mrs Firth had to perceive, without significance; he was gazing out of the window, the deepening sunset light casting shadows on his face that showed it as more handsome than she remembered. She asked, struck by the recollection: 'How come you to be staying with the people at Woodston? How can Miss Tilney be your niece?'

'Perhaps she is not exactly that? Only that my sister married her uncle? My sister, you may remember; you were very friendly with her during – that season in Bath, you know.'

'Oh yes, I remember,' agreed Mrs Firth, who did not. 'A most sweet girl. Well then, how strange it is that we two should have met again after so long. I hope it makes you happy.'

He bowed, his expression not overjoyed. 'The coincidence is extreme. I am glad we have established it.' She waited for him to add that he was also glad to have established, or renewed, his relationship with herself. She would see to it that he did. She took up her netting needle to indicate her composure and ease in his company. He roused himself from some reverie to ask:

'And you; you have kept up some association with the Tilney family? You have met them – in town, or in Bath – and visited the Abbey, since the – episode we mentioned; you knew the old General? You have spoken as if you did not.'

Mrs Firth hesitated. She did not wish to announce that she had arrived at the Abbey merely in the train of her brother who was engaged in work there; but it might be incautious to claim acquaintance with the family, when Miss Tilney and the Woodston set could not confirm it. She inspected her netting for a few moments and then replied, lightly:

'Well, you know, one meets people, here and there, now and then, without keeping count; I suppose among my friends they come and go.' If this did not tally with her description of her lonely life she did not recognise that. And Mr Morland, after an interval of reflection, rose to his feet and spoke as if he had come to a decision:

'I will stay here, then, for the present, if the household can accommodate me. I am much interested in the matter of the old chapel; but also I feel, I cannot say why, that there may be some mischief afoot; or even, danger?'

Mrs Firth did not know what he meant by mischief; it could not apply to herself. Now were her intentions towards Mr Morland, as he would discover, in the least to his danger.

'Indeed I hope that you will stay,' she said, plying her needle.

The disaster of James Morland's first and only love affair had not blighted his life but re-directed it. He was broken-hearted but not embittered; he became more devout, and from his humble beginnings in the church, toiled long and patiently; he earned the respect of the authorities, was appointed to an Oxford fellowship, and achieved more than he could have, had he been cumbered with wife and children. He consoled himself with no such reflection, but thanked God for his undeserved merits. From his encounter with the lively and lovely Isabella Thorpe he had acquired a sympathy with women and their weaknesses that few bachelors attain. This evening, he pitied her, finding her so much the same; a dormant sadness had been roused in him but no regret. During the years, as he visited Woodston, he had avoided the Abbey, since it was the handsome young Captain Tilney twenty years ago who had a fatally counter-attracting effect on the lovely Isabella; but now, after so long, James Morland did not see why they should not all be on amicable terms. He was well disposed towards Mrs Firth; it was beneath him to admit that he might have had, in that direction, a fortunate escape.

8

By this time it was becoming noticeable to everyone except John Thorpe, that for all his talk and energy John Thorpe had accomplished precisely nothing. His latest project was to paint with whitewash various arrows and symbols on wall corners, then change his mind and tell the attendant garden boy to wash them off again. He was still productive of ideas, and hailed Mr Morland as the latter was crossing the cloister:

'James, I say! Here! I must have your opinion of this—'

James Morland, in his previous acquaintance with Miss Thorpe, had known her brother, who had been a college friend. Since then they had scarcely met, but each was willing – from charity on the one side and indifference on the other – to resume a form of friendship now that coincidence had reunited them. As James approached John proclaimed: 'I have thought of the cellars. I could make a way through to *underneath* the chapel – Come, I must show you.' He was busily lighting a lantern.

'I do not see the virtue of being below the chapel – I do not suppose it would have a crypt; and if so, it will have been filled in—'

'How do you know? Try to be thorough. Be like me – I never leave an avenue unexplored. Now, at *this* end is the late lamented General's wine cellar, and a spacious thing it is, the old tippler. But down *this* way – Mind your head – is a passage leading along to a root cellar – Careful, there are puddles – but a gap that I cannot account for—'

Taking John Thorpe's word for this, since the lantern shed light enough for the leader only, Mr Morland followed him like Agag, delicately. As they proceeded, he thought to say:

'I was speaking to Mrs Firth last evening; it seems she had not recognised me.'

'Who – Bella? No, I suppose she would not. You look such a sad dog, compared with what you were in our happy youth. – Do you imagine we have walked as far as one hundred yards now?'

'Twenty yards, perhaps. She does not appear very happy herself.'

'Oh, forty yards at least – Can you hear anything?'

They stood still. James Morland said: 'Something dripping . . .'

'Well, water, obviously. The General's wine casks yield no largesse, you can be sure of that. I quite agree with you; my sister is a disagreeable hag.'

James Morland forbore to correct that quotation. 'I understood, that she is not well provided for; did her husband not—'

'Her husband did nothing. She should not have married that useless Firth and I told her so.' That this admonition had been given after the marriage John Thorpe found irrelevant. 'Now, why should the chapel not have had a crypt, can you tell me that?'

'Just, that a chapel of this moderate size would have had no need—'

'Unless they filled it with dead abbots – or used it as a wine cellar. Now look,' he went on in rising excitement, 'here is a thing I had not noticed. Here, where the square stones form a protruding edge – I swear it could be the corner of the chapel foundations!'

James Morland had just time to identify the irregularity in the wall of the passage, and to concur, when John Thorpe in his exaltation swung the lantern so that it hit the wall and was extinguished. He swore; the two gentlemen stood in the dripping darkness. 'Well,' said John Thorpe unabashed, 'I will leave something – my kerchief, would do – here, so that we find the spot again.'

'If we can find our way out again,' said James Morland with pious calm. 'I can feel my way – Follow me, will you . . .' He ran his fingers along the wall, noting as he did so that no wine or root cellar worth its name would be so damp. John Thorpe, after planting his kerchief, suddenly produced a piercing and terrible: 'Whoo-hooo!' which echoed along the invisible passages and made James Morland start violently, slipping on an uneven stone; his calm inhibited him from comment, but he had an unpleasant shock which made him grateful to see daylight begin to gleam ahead and give way to comforting sunlight.

'*That* frightened you,' remarked John Thorpe with satisfaction.

James Morland was not sorry to make his way to the library and settle with a book by the sunny window. Rather than ponder the depths of the Abbey cellars he turned his mind to Mrs Firth and to her brother's disobliging reference to her. It was possible that her poverty – if her husband indeed had not provided for her – had been a sore trial; of the details of her life he was ignorant – what had she in the way of a home, when she was there? Insecurity could undermine the strongest character. He had reached this preliminary thesis when, by a strange chance, Roland Firth looked into the library:

'Mr Morland – I am sorry, you are reading—'

'Not attentively. Did you need me for something?'

'Only – when you have a spare moment – If I could ask you for some advice?'

'For any I can give,' said James, not displeased. He liked

this diligent and modest boy – perhaps, at the moment, the more for his contrast with John Thorpe. He knew too that Roland aspired to ordination; in giving advice here, James would be on more familiar ground. 'What is troubling you?'

Roland seated himself at a small ornamental table in the window and laid down a letter and a leather bag that chinked. 'I had a letter,' he began, 'from Mr Ballard. My employer; Charles's father. It is not, indeed, in his own hand – it is written by the chief clerk in the foundry office. It encloses an amount of money.' Roland unfolded the page and read aloud: 'Mr Ballard hereby remits Mr Firth's emoluments and pocket money for that extravagant sprig believed to be still in Mr Firth's charge.' Glancing up to catch a glance of faint surprise from Mr Morland he added: 'This will have been dictated by Mr Ballard – this is his way, with Charles . . .' And, reading on: 'Also as Mr Ballard is relieved of the expense of the two aforementioned in his house, he retains only the amount required for the feeding of the yapping Xerxes and remits a small contribution towards the keep of the af'mtd two, ignorant as he yet is of who is bearing that expense.' Looking up, Roland appealed: 'You see my difficulty, sir?'

'. . . Would you explain the classical allusion?'

'Oh; Xerxes is Charles's dog.' Folding the letter, Roland sighed. 'Mr Ballard is generous – everyone is being generous to us – but I see no way of . . . I cannot approach Miss Tilney – for Charles and I are, after all, living here at her expense – How can I offer her money?' he implored.

'I too am here at her charge,' said James Morland, 'in so far as she represents her family. But—'

'But you are a *guest*, sir, she invited you. I cannot yet explain how Charles and I came to be here—'

'I can assure you,' James Morland told him, 'that Paulina is happy to have both of you here. I do not believe that the thought of expense has entered her head.'

He observed that Roland blushed; lowering his head as if

aware of that and hoping to conceal it, the young man began to gather the coins from his wallet; some few he piled and set aside; he murmured: 'My own salary, I can fairly take. Then I can lay the same amount to Charles's account – but what does he need pocket money for, here? Everything is provided . . . I could hand the money to Mr Benson – or Brook – but it would seem officious, or worse, to do so behind Miss Tilney's back . . .'

'Nor would you return it to Mr Ballard?' suggested James Morland. Roland's astonished gaze admitted an impossibility there. Sighing again he returned to his allocations, removing the greater part of the money he had named as his and saying in a suddenly cheerful aside:

'At any rate I need feel no embarrassment in sharing my own portion with my mother.'

This caught James Morland's interest, the more so as he had been reflecting upon Mr Firth's mother since his interview with her. 'Mrs Firth is not embarrassed by the handling of money?'

'She is embarrassed, in another sense, by her lack of it,' said Mrs Firth's son with candour. 'She would freely accept all of this that so embarrasses me, could she get her hands on it.'

James Morland had witnessed, in what he had observed of the relations between mother and son, that young Firth could display a mixture of deference and mild mockery – neither of which his mother appreciated. Roland's expression at this moment was both rueful and tolerant. James asked: 'Has she been at great expense on your behalf? You now hope to repay her?'

'I would dearly like,' said Roland with vehemence, 'to be able to support my mother altogether. I have watched her struggles and straits ever since my father died, and to see her settled in comfort would be as great a relief to me as to her.'

'And, with that relief, what would you devote yourself to?'

71

Roland frowned, disconsolate. 'Oh, I do not know. I should like to take orders. And I do enjoy teaching – or, tutoring, which is all I have so far attempted; I do not know that I would like a crowd of noisy boys at a school. If I were truly free – that is, with no responsibilities – I would like to travel abroad and write – I do not know what; not poetry I think – but essays, and the more serious kind of novel . . .' His face, as he uttered these notions was boyish and half sulky. James Morland summarised it: He cannot tell what he wants, since he is not 'truly free' – of what? Of his mother?

'You are young yet; you will have time to find your way—'

'I shall come of age in only a few weeks. And then, I should like to repay – in some fashion – my uncle who has spent so much on fees and so on, for me. – But I am taking up your time.'

'Not at all – I am grateful that you confide in me.' James would certainly bear this young man in mind, should the question of clerical preferment arise and should James have any influence in the future. Roland's future, however, was to be determined only by Roland; any suggestion at this point would be premature. 'I wonder if you would like me to consult Mr Benson for you, and perhaps offer to hold Mr Ballard's money meanwhile, in case the household may have a use for it? If that should arise, we might then discuss it with Paulina.'

'I would be glad, sir, of your advice and support . . . What had you in mind, in speaking of a use . . .?'

'For instance, supposing your uncle – Mr Thorpe – were to wreak any damage to the Abbey during his operations, this could stand as an insurance that we could remedy things without troubling Colonel Tilney? What would Mr Ballard think of that?'

'He would think it pretty good sense,' said Roland. 'And so do I. But do you suppose Uncle John is capable . . .'

'We do not know yet,' said James Morland between amusement and apprehensiveness, 'of what your Uncle John is capable.'

John Thorpe's recent underground explorations had aroused fresh and skilled interest in the neighbourhood. The stonemason and his men, with lanterns and picks, descended in search of the damp passage, which assuredly should not have been there. Nor did it seem to be; John Thorpe's insistence that his kerchief marked the spot lost force when the kerchief was not found. All the same, there was a discovery, and a discrepancy, somewhere. And, the dripping of water softly mocked them when they stood silent.

The cellars of the modern wing of the Abbey were in perfect order. The General's father had seen to that. But clear of those cellars, if not beneath the ruined chapel, some area had been left, with the slippery passage leading to or through it; none of the Abbey staff or residents had suspected it; John Thorpe was certain he and James Morland had entered by the steps leading down from the root cellar passage, and walked straight ahead for 'about half a mile'. James Morland appended:

'For perhaps fifty yards. And, the passage may well have curved; we could not guarantee that it was straight, though we did not turn any corners.'

Finally it was the Abbey builders, with their picks and levers, who selected a point at which to broach the wall – Not where John Thorpe bade them, but as they were guided by the dripping of water – and they broke through into a space wherein the water threaded in a trickle through tumbled stone; they scrambled about with their lanterns and Tom cried:

'Here we have it. There was an old well. It'd be fed by a spring into t'bottom – Then a lot of earth and stone fell, and the well were to overflow till it ran out – back there in the dark might be an outlet, like a crack—'

73

'So we are now in my passage!' proclaimed John Thorpe.

'Like as not; ay, it runs some way up yonder, but to this way 'tis blocked with earth – May be, it's to be shifted – Well, lads, we must dig a bit and get it tidied up – Good thing it's not leaked over into the house cellars. Now let us to our dinner; we'm all tired.'

They turned to crawl back through their hole, pursued by John Thorpe crying: 'But where is my kerchief!'

Tom looked back to call kindly: 'Come, sir, we'll buy you another!' The men laughed, the sound rumbling eerily into the darkness beyond the lanterns. John Thorpe was not appeased.

He found an audience in Roland and Charles, who were sitting in the cloister corner with their books. Roland had forbidden Charles to take part in the subterranean expedition, and Charles, little as he had to spend money on here, had profited by the gift of pocket money to the extent of resuming his lessons with more ardour; at present, it was not only books that enabled him to feel he was 'living in a special world'; buried chapels had their glamour, and John Thorpe pleaded their cause:

'They laugh at me when I tap at their walls with a hammer, but you should see how they laid about them down there – smashing their way through willy-nilly, not listening to a word of mine – All they cared about was those cellars, that they might get a little wet – And I had found something of real interest – an old well; who needs a well, underground? It must have had a *head* – Where, and why? And why for G—'s sake that old passage? For all we know that chapel had an even older one below it – or the passage was a secret way out—'

'Why a secret?' inquired Charles.

'After the Reformation, the Abbey could have been a shelter for recusants?' suggested Roland.

'I do not care what it was for. I am going to find out what there *is* of it now. If those beefy labourers start shifting all

the earth down there they will block up the end of the
passage and do G— knows what other harm. I know what I
shall do; I shall find the head of that well and start excavating from there.' He strode off muttering: 'A dowser. That is
what I shall need. A dowser – Do you know of one, ma'am?'
he demanded of Miss Tilney who happened to be coming
out of the long window of the library.

'A . . .? I expect one of the gardeners might help you,'
she said, drawing up on tiptoes as Mr Thorpe almost collided into her. Roland noted how graceful she was in her
every movement, but lowered his eyes quickly as she came
on to ask him and Charles:

'What do you suppose he wishes to dowse?'

Charles tried to explain; she exclaimed: 'A well, near the
site of the chapel – if indeed Mr Thorpe has located
the site . . .' She was laughing, but then asked Roland
seriously:

'Do you think Mr Thorpe at all knows what – that is, is
he entirely . . . reliable?'

Hoping he sounded reliable himself, Roland told her: 'I
think Mr Morland has wondered about that, and has a
scheme to guard against any mishap.'

'Well then. I am glad Uncle James is here. You see, I have
seen so little of Mr Thorpe and would hesitate to question
him.'

Roland almost warned her that questions to Mr Thorpe
would yield a wide variety of answers, but did not wish to
trouble her; she smiled and passed on, and he and Charles,
who had risen when she approached, sat down to their
books. Charles observed:

'I am sorry for Miss Tilney really, that she has us all here
when she might have the Abbey to herself. She told me that
she usually does, when she comes in the summer.'

Paulina, as her uncle had assured Roland, was not sorry
to have this studious pair here. She was pleased too that
Uncle James was making a long stay; she felt he deserved a

rest, after thė farewells in his Camden parish and all his hard work in London. The expense of their keep she had not thought to consider. Mr Thorpe, as she said, she rarely saw; he did not favour the dinner table with his company. She had not yet lost faith in his creation of a chapel – only, he seemed to go in a roundabout way to it. Paulina was aware that Mrs Wight thought it suitable that Paulina behave, on this occasion, as the lady of the house; that was not unpleasant, and the visitors did not require much entertainment; chats in the housekeeper's room were not prevented. It was only Mrs Firth whom Paulina found difficult. She was restless, yet did not respond to Paulina's overtures; she was often alone, yet had a way of wandering into sight if Paulina happened to be in conversation with Uncle James or with Mr Firth. The latter opportunities were few, since Mr Firth was so much with Charles, which Paulina applauded; she could perceive that his influence on Charles was wholly beneficial. Yet, she would have enjoyed making the closer acquaintance of Mr Firth; he had a sensitivity and humour that she responded to, or felt that she would, had his mother not been so often in a doorway or on the skyline. What, Paulina would wonder, did the lady want?

Mrs Firth, just now, knew very well what she wanted. Roland had given her Mr Ballard's money – keeping some for himself, though what had he to spend it on, here, where everything was provided? Mrs Firth had far better use for it. As all ladies know, the gleam of gold renders all one's clothes dingy and frayed; Mrs Firth had nothing fit to wear, as soon as she had the means of correcting that condition.

But, how? The nearest town was not, as she remembered it from her journey here, very fashionable; but then, she had been in haste to hire a carriage, and tired too; besides, it was not 'fashionable' dress that she wanted, but something elegant but sober, as befitted the wife of a Canon of a London cathedral. For her limited acquaintance with ladies of that status, Mrs Firth had considered them as plump, neat and dowdy; but there was no reason to emulate them; for the first time in many years she was inspired with the wish to excel; she would be modest, distinguished and . . . Well, elegant.

'Miss Tilney,' she said at the dinner table rather sharply, so as not to sound like one asking a favour, 'would it be possible for me to be conveyed into the town to do a little shopping?'

'Certainly, Mrs Firth. When would you like to go? Would you like me to accompany you? I could show you some of the country, and point out the best shops—'

'Thank you, but I know the best shops when I see them. I would like to go in the morning, if that is convenient.'

'Certainly it is, Mrs Firth.'

9

A trim little chaise appeared at the front door of the Abbey for Mrs Firth. Also appeared her son Roland followed by Charles. 'Mama,' he asked, 'would there not be a place beside you for Charles? He very much wants to buy some small things in the town.' Behind Roland, on the doorsteps, now appeared James Morland, smiling approval of the suggestion; otherwise, Mrs Firth would have told her son emphatically that she was not disposed to cumber herself with this clumsy boy about the town; as it was she said coldly:

'I suppose so, so long as he does not keep me waiting.'

In the event Charles did not; Mrs Firth was a full two hours in the town after bidding him be ready to depart in one hour without fail. As they drove thither she and he engaged in no conversation. When Charles had begun with:

'This is most kind of you, ma'am. You see, my father has sent me some pocket money—' she cut him off with:

'You are fortunate, I am sure.'

After that Charles spoke to the groom who drove them and Mrs Firth pursued her own plans. The town's shops, as she had supposed, offered no wide choice; she had decided during the drive on a demure sort of bonnet for church, two gowns to be made from silver-grey or dark rose, and a fine muslin, perhaps with lilac sprigs; then there must be gloves, kerchiefs, slippers . . .

Her downfall was caused by a pretty little cross set with seed pearls that she noticed in the window of a jeweller's. That she must have. With it went a fine silver chain which was also essential. Silver chains Mrs Firth had, in her jewel case, but she was afraid they were too heavy to go through the ring of the cross. After that, she was dismayed to find that she could afford only one length of poplin – and having paid for that, there was not a bonnet within her means; she was lucky to arrive back at the chaise with more than a pair of gloves. It put her in no mood to tolerate the patient Charles on the drive back to the Abbey.

'Put your parcels under your feet,' she commanded him. 'You have left no room for mine.' As he bent to slide his small packages out of her way, pulling up his inert left foot in his haste, she added: 'Oh, do not make yourself so awkward. You make a display of your lameness, to gain pity. Here, you can hold this larger parcel of mine on your lap. What have you been buying, may I ask?'

'Ma'am, I wanted new steel pens, for myself and Mr Firth. And a notebook to write out my Greek verbs. And I bought a present for Miss Tilney.'

'How absurd. You are far too young to give presents to ladies. She will think you unmannerly and forward.'

Anxious, Charles told her: 'It is only a small picture, in a gilt frame. The lady in the shop thought it would be quite acceptable—'

'Then she knew no better, either. And I expect it was expensive. You are lucky to have a rich father who spoils you.'

'Yes ma'am. It is a picture of a little girl with a kitten in her arms,' Charles mentioned in the dull tone of one already disappointed.

'How very childish. But then, so she is, is she not. She has

79

the audacity to behave like the queen of the place but no one pays heed to her, which she does not notice.'

'Miss Tilney has been very kind,' murmured Charles. The groom at this point, perceiving a large loose stone on the road, steered the off wheel of the chaise across it; his passengers were given a jolt that nearly unseated them and turned Mrs Firth's wrath against the groom for the remainder of the drive.

Charles absorbed the effect of Mrs Firth's manner to him only slowly. No one had been cruel to him before. His father had been rough – Mr Firth strict – his mother often nagged; people laughed at him or ignored him; but he had never felt the naked blade of malice. He could not understand it.

Mrs Firth had been irritated from the start by this boy who had come between her and her son, and at present she was willing to wish everyone excepting James Morland off the face of the earth. She was resentful of each member of her immediate circle, but it was not to her credit that she chose the weakest of them on whom to vent her annoyance. It did not occur to her that Charles was not as weak as he, to her, appeared.

While this inharmonious pair was out, there had been much activity at the Abbey. The masons and gang had been attacking the underground mystery, with much battering and hallooing and lantern-flashing; John Thorpe, since they obeyed none of his orders – or indeed heard them – had retired to the surface and busied himself with tracing the course of his find, or conjecturing it, and looking important. The water diviner had been sent for, to a nearby village, and presently he arrived, driving a donkey cart piled with the brushwood and scouring stone that was his normal trading stock. He was a young man who whistled between his teeth as he listened to John Thorpe's instructions.

'A well, eh? Nay, it'd need to be a spring.'

'There *is* a well. We – I found the shaft. Get to work, man.'

'And where shall I do that, master?'

'Far from me be it to tell you your job. If you know it.'

The young man twirled his hazel rod in a casual fashion that John Thorpe found provoking. He was about to send the bumpkin away in disgust, but there arrived now several of the toilers from below, faces and arms plastered with clay.

'Bernard, good day,' cried their leader to the dowser. 'Now we've found a spring under there and we want to trap it. Likely its source is outside the walls – a few yards – this way—' he pointed his thumb. They all looked about them, at the sunny and impeccable Abbey grounds. Bernard, whistling, strolled along by the wall, through the stillroom, out again and through Mrs Wight's fine laundry, remarking only: 'Daft place for a spring . . . Might try the garden . . .'

John Thorpe, perforce following, saw the hazel rod twitch a little, and decided the man was doing that purposely. Along the side of the drying green they went, and round the end of the high yew hedge. Here the dowser paused, wiping his brow. His task, whatever John Thorpe thought, required an effort of concentration. The rod was hanging limp. Tom said doubtfully: 'I reckon it'd be more to the left – westward, like.'

'Ay; 'tis drying up hereabouts . . . What's been here?' Bernard inquired idly, pointing his free hand along the ground.

'Here! Nothing but grass—'

'I meant, this darker green – see? There's a-bin a wall; a wide one—'

'Ay, but that'd be old; before the new side of the Abbey was even built—'

John Thorpe leapt forward. 'A wall? An *old* wall? I see – it comes under the hedge there – It must be part of the old chapel!' He glared about him, for further traces. One of the builders, scratching his head, remarked in the most incidental fashion:

'Might be. Down there—' he tilted his head – 'we broke

81

through past that well shaft and broke into an empty place like a cave – full of rubble it was, but it'd a bit of a groined ceiling—'

'Why did you not tell me at once!' cried John Thorpe. 'You stupid yokels – We have found the old chapel!'

Since the water diviner had accidentally discovered a buried wall, and the water workers had accidentally discovered the crypt, it was perhaps a little vainglorious of John Thorpe to claim that his own efforts had been rewarded. But stirred by his triumph he instantly summoned every gardener and spade within call, and set about hacking up the turf of the drying green and rooting out a section of yew hedge, to uncover the wall that he was now convinced to be there, just where he had known the site of the chapel to be, from the Woodston engraving and from his own calculations. It must be admitted that throughout his work the weather had been sunny, and the shadow of the yew hedge had fallen across the colouring of the grass; today, by some chance, the sky was grey – and now, as the digging began, so did the rain. The builders had returned to their task, after establishing with the dowser's authority that the spring below was no great matter. They decided to conduct it by channel and pipe into a deep cleft in the limestone that should drain it away with no harm to the fabric of the Abbey cellars or offices. As they laboured they paid no regard to the cavity with the groined roof; crypt it might be, but if the lunatic above wanted it, he could surely dig down to it from his chapel? So they shovelled an amount of rubble into the old shaft, slapped mortar over it, and left a couple of their new breaches in the walls open, in case some ventilation would help; they agreed that they had done a tidy job. It must be admitted too that, to this day, no one has understood how the original builders of the Abbey – or someone at an earlier time – had sunk a well just there; nor who had made that long passage past it, and why; nor how the General's father came to complete his building of the quadrangle without discovering all this. There may have been some simple explanation but it would have taken more ingenuity than John Thorpe's to supply it. Today, John Thorpe was as pleased with himself, having discovered one wall of the chapel, as if he had the whole chapel discovered and rebuilt.

He came to the dinner table, late, and with earth on his fingernails but with a great deal to say. '. . . So you see I was quite right. My men have scraped bare a length of stone blocks – as big as elephants – that must have been the side wall. Cromwell or whoever it was, saw that it would give too much trouble to dig them out, so he left them. Lucky for me.'

'Not so lucky,' Mr Morland remarked, 'for the yew hedge that you have torn out. It too may have dated back to Cromwell's time.'

'Oh James, why need you throw cold water? It was only an old hedge – too high and thick, anyhow.'

'And, speaking of water, do I understand that the men who saw to the drainage underground, also found what might be the crypt of the chapel?'

'Might be? Why are you so gloomy? There it was, with a groined roof—'

'I might rather have expected barrel vaulting.'

'Well, whatever you expected, there it is for you – You must go down and see it. There are your coffins and the bones of abbots and all the rest of it.' With a wave of his hand, John obliterated the suspicion that the floor of his chapel and the location of the discovered chamber had not been brought yet into juxtaposition.

'I shall go down and see it,' assented James Morland, 'when the work is fully completed.'

'Well, and that will not be long hence, now we have made a beginning.'

Paulina said to Roland, who sat beside her: 'I remember that my grandfather was particularly proud of the old yew hedge. My sister and I once climbed up inside it to make ourselves a tree-house – But a gardener saw us, and told him, and we were sent for to the library for a severe talking-to.'

'*Well,* the gardeners will not sneak on you to the General now,' declared John Thorpe overhearing. 'Unless of course he is sitting up in his coffin in the crypt, waiting to catch you.'

'*John,*' complained Mrs Firth, 'do not be so morbid. You will frighten this boy.'

Charles looked from side to side as if for the boy referred to; 'Me, ma'am? I do not think the General will have been buried in that crypt. I have seen his tomb in the churchyard.'

'It might take more than a tomb to restrain the General,' said John Thorpe. 'Did you yourself not hear him, James, hooting like an owl, while we're exploring down yonder?'

At the idea of her grandfather hooting like an owl, Paulina could not help laughing. Roland joined in, captivated by the dimples in her cheeks; and Charles laughed in sympathy. Mrs Firth said coldly:

'I do not think it reverent, to laugh at such serious matters.'

Everyone obediently became serious. She peeped under her lashes to see what effect her dignified reproof had had on James Morland; his expression was grave enough. He was asking:

'Do you suppose, John, that the other foundation walls of the chapel are still in place? There would, then, be one parallel to today's revelation?'

'Oh, definitely. It will run under that stillroom, but its side walls are only of modern blocks – we shall soon have it down.'

'And does Frederick Tilney know about all this?'

'Of course. He gave me full authority. Besides, he is abroad.'

Paulina interposed: 'He may not be for much longer, Mr

Thorpe. I did not tell you, but I had a letter from my sister today; she says they may return to England sooner than they had intended.'

'Then we must finish the work even faster,' cried John, raising his glass before quaffing his wine with vigorous purpose.

Her sister's letter had been much on Paulina's mind since it came. Annabella Tilney had written:

'. . . and the château was so hot and inconvenient and the roads so bad and the town so crowded when we reached the coast, and now we have moved to the mountains Mama thinks the thin air gives her the headache, she has not been well for all this time and I am frantic – My dear Polly it is *your* turn. If we come back to England will you *please* come and bear her company, for then I could go to Scotland with the Harringtons?'

This appeal Paulina would not refuse. She said now, turning again to Roland:

'My sister would like me to leave here, and go to bear my mother company.'

'But you must not do that!' exclaimed Roland before he could check himself.

'Indeed she must!' said Mrs Firth, with a vigour equal to John's. 'No daughter can defy a mother's wishes.' This fervour did attract James Morland's attention; he glanced at Mrs Firth in slight surprise. She hoped it had not sounded – though it was true – that she wished to be rid of Miss Tilney. She smiled kindly at the girl, with whom at present she was in an awkward position. Rather than inquire of Miss Tilney she had asked Mrs Wight whether there was a good dressmaker nearby; Mrs Wight had assured her that the Abbey's chief sewing-maid was an excellent dressmaker; Mrs Firth had replied: 'Oh, I do not think a domestic would be good enough!' whereat Mrs Wight had said, coolly, that Miss Tilney in that case might advise Mrs Firth – who was now committed either to seeking out a dressmaker for herself in

85

this rustic desert, or to grappling, herself, with the new poplin. For this predicament, naturally, she blamed Miss Tilney. But she had not intended to antagonise the girl – much less, to lower herself in James Morland's eyes. Touching the seed pearl cross at her throat, she said at large:

'I am afraid the weather is changing; I hope we shall not have a long spell of rain.'

'But Mr Thorpe in that case may take shelter in his crypt,' Roland suggested. With a roar of laughter John Thorpe pushed back his chair and left the table, adding:

'I should not long subsist on a diet of abbots' bones.'

Charles at this gave an involuntary shudder of distaste, and Mrs Firth said sweetly to him:

'Yes, I knew all this talk of the crypt frightened you – but of course, you will not be allowed down there, with your afflictions. Do not worry.'

Charles did not answer but his lips set in a line of unusual petulance. Roland, watching, wondered that Mrs Firth seemed determined to show such lack of tact in dealing with Charles; James Morland too wondered why she was not kinder to the boy. As the meal ended, he went to the window to look out at the rain; the clouds were heavy and the trees dripping; there would be no roses in today's sunset. Mrs Firth joined him.

'I could wish my brother would more often stay away from the table. I am afraid he is somewhat uncouth in his manners.'

'His enthusiasm makes him regardless at times. But he is making progress at last in his project.'

'And what harm may that do? Knocking down walls . . .'

James Morland smiled. 'As I remember, your brother's plans when he was young often exceeded his final achievements.'

'But that was in his youth. We all hope to grow wiser and more restrained as the years pass.' She sighed. 'I know that life has taught me moderation and . . . gratitude. I am not

86

at all the same as the giddy and thoughtless girl you once knew.'

She felt that he studied her face for a moment, but he did not reply. 'I am sorry that Mrs Tilney is not well,' he resumed. 'If Paulina is to go to London I shall offer myself as escort.'

'Oh! – Oh? I suppose she is young to travel alone. That is another thing my life has forced upon me: To be self-reliant. It does not seem Mrs Tilney lacks attention; I fancy she is a spoilt and selfish woman. Is she truly delicate?'

'I believe she does not enjoy good health.'

'Then, in that small way, I am more favoured than she. I am never ill.'

By such subtle stipulations Mrs Firth strove to recommend herself to James Morland. Had she known it, she was beginning to appeal to him – Not, to rouse his admiration, but to evoke his pity. She was protesting, he felt, too much; that is, she was longing to be rescued from the giddy thoughtlessness that had lingered from her girlhood; with the right sort of guidance, and a measure of security, she might mature into a happier woman. It was merciful that he said none of this to her, but he gave her a not unsympathetic smile before saying:

'Of that I am glad. Now, shall we join the others, and ask Paulina to play for us? We may not have many more opportunities.'

Of that last, Mrs Firth was glad. She had no musical training nor aptitude and had suffered from having to listen to Miss Tilney's monopoly of the pianoforte. On this occasion her suffering was extended, so much that she could barely remain in her chair, since Miss Tilney persuaded Charles to sing. He proved to have a clear treble voice, and to have learnt at home two arias by Handel. Roland, applauding with the others, said:

'Why, Charles, I did not know you could sing!'

'Well, sir, I have had no need to do so, while I was with

you. I used to have music lessons – two or three years ago; but I gave them up when I took to serious study.'

Mrs Firth, who had not applauded, pointed out:

'You should sing while you can; soon, your voice might alter and drop, as you grow – Unless of course you remain stunted for all your life.'

The boy's face took on that same stiff sulkiness; Mrs Firth was convinced that he had been over-encouraged, and allowed to think too well of himself in view of his disabilities. She told herself that she wished sincerely to help him; in a strange way she felt sympathy for him: She and he must both learn to rise above themselves and become more unselfish; if she found this, in fitting herself for James Morland, a strenuous effort, she liked to feel that someone else was submitted to the same ordeal. She did not think herself at all vindictive; it was simply that one must suffer in order to progress. Did Charles Ballard but know it, she was setting him a fine example. She wished now that she had brought up Roland to have what a moral book she had borrowed from the Abbey library called 'a higher sense of values.'

James Morland, as he continued to reflect upon Isabella Firth and her character, felt increasingly obliged to rise above himself and judge according to a higher sense of values. Pious as he was, his personal life was suspended in a form of naïveté; if one perceived what was best to be done, then it must be done, even against one's inclinations. This principle had stood him in good stead throughout his life so far; but his life had been uncomplicated by women of Isabella Firth's stamp. As she sought higher values in order to attract him, he could not help seeing that those values in her still required much gentle correction. His heart sank but his spirit rose as he came to adjure himself that it might be his Christian duty to marry her.

10

John Thorpe was faced with a rebellion from Mrs Wight: the smaller stillroom was in use and she could not empty its shelves and slabs; would Mr Thorpe kindly dig somewhere else. 'As if I were digging merely for my own pleasure!' he grumbled. 'But the old witch will see soon enough that the wall of the chapel must lie there. When I have uncovered the foundation wall to the opposite . . .'

In the continuing rain, he would have preferred to be knocking down walls under cover; nor in this frustration had he the heart to resume his search for the crypt. 'Those fellows have been blocking up passages and knocking holes, just as it pleased them. I cannot find the turn of our passage, James – where I found that section of underground wall, you remember? It might have been important. They have left a hogget-hole too narrow to crawl through – Hey, why do we not send this shrimp down to go through? He is as small as a chimney-sweep's boy!'

'John,' said his sister, 'do not be unkind. Poor Charles can not help being so puny.'

Because the weather, while not cold, was so gloomy, a fire had been lit in the modern marble fireplace of the drawing room, and there the company was gathered today. Mrs Firth and James Morland had been sitting one on either side of it, he with his book and she with her netting-box; as if, she had noted, they were a peacefully married couple. Now he rose and began to pace the room, slowly, pausing to gaze out of the window. Roland and Charles were at a far table, Roland giving Charles a dictation; Miss Tilney in a corner was sewing.

'Roland,' complained Mrs Firth, 'must you talk on and on like that? You are disturbing Mr Morland.'

'Very well,' Roland replied. 'Charles, read over your work now, and correct any mistakes.'

Silence followed; Mr Morland did not return to his chair. Mrs Firth, glancing round the room, for a moment remembered how happy she had been, not long ago, to fancy herself mistress of the Abbey. There could be few rooms as pleasant as this, in which to dispose oneself.—But then, watching James Morland, she reminded herself of the large house in London near to St Paul's. She knew where her heart truly lay.

The silence had been mostly occasioned by the departure of John Thorpe; all too soon he came bursting back into the room to declare:

'Well, the rain is slackening, and these men need something to occupy them. We shall start excavating the north wall – we know where it lies – It will take off a corner of that bowling green, you know, and we shall begin by knocking down that silly little pavilion affair, it will take but a moment – Here, little chimney-sweep, here are some balls for you to play with.' He slung on to the table, with a crash, a net of bowls, and slammed out of the room again.

Roland remarked to Miss Tilney: 'I expect your grandfather took a pride too in his bowling green.'

She smiled slightly, shaking her head. 'Charles,' she asked, 'do you know how to play bowls?' She laid down her sewing and unfastened the net. Charles took up one of the bowls, saying:

'They are heavy. I had a heavy ball like this, and I had to

use it to exercise my left hand.' His left hand sagged under the weight.

'But these, you see, are biased – that is, they will not run smoothly as a normal ball . . .' She moved to the end of the room and rolled the jack slowly across the polished boards. If it came to disturbing Mr Morland, thought Mrs Firth, this girl showed an outrageous audacity; now Roland and Charles were both beside her, each hefting a bowl.

'I suppose,' reflected Mrs Firth aloud, 'children must be allowed to play noisy games when they cannot be out of doors.'

Mr Morland, still at the window, observed: 'The rain is not slackening; I believe John was exerting his will on the elements. Miss Tilney,' he added, 'it seems we have visitors.'

The sound of wheels could be heard from the gravel driveway. Paulina, after watching the wobbling progress of Charles's bowl until it thudded into the wainscot, joined her uncle, Roland following. A carriage had halted, the coachman peering through the rain as if uncertain, while a manservant jumped from the box to speak to a lady who peered from the carriage window. She was plump and frowning, in black bonnet and shawl. As the door of the carriage opened and she began to descend, Paulina cried:

'It is one of our carriages – It is Nana – Mrs Grant – our old nurse – Oh, what can be the matter?' She ran from the room so fast that in a moment she had fled through the front door and was out in the rain, clinging to the plump lady whose arms were round her; James Morland and Roland consulted each other only with a brief startled glance before hurrying out to the hallway; there they met Paulina as she returned, rain and tears streaking her face, to fling her arms round James Morland, sobbing:

'My Mama is ill – very ill – they say she is *dying*—'

Raising her head from her uncle's shoulder she cast an appealing look at Roland, who felt that his face had become

91

white with the shock. But even in her own alarm, Miss Tilney could say:

'Nana – Come indoors; you are wet.' Then, with an attempt at trembling calm: 'We must go – to London – at *once.*'

In little more than an hour's time Paulina was gone.

James Morland thought it better not to accompany her. She could not have a more fitting escort than her old nurse; and Mrs Grant's tidings that Mrs Tilney was suffering from cholera made it all too probable that the journey was towards a deathbed, which was a matter for the family; James had no acquaintance with the Tilneys now and would not wish to intrude. He sent a messenger to Woodston, in case the Reverend Henry had not also been told of his sister-in-law's plight, then set himself to wait for further news.

Anxiety prevailed at the Abbey. Mrs Firth said: 'Would it not be better for us to go away?' but James Morland said that he saw no reason to do so, yet at any rate. 'Well I agree with you,' she answered. 'Besides, I have nowhere to go. It is hard for you, I expect, to picture the helplessness of the homeless. I am so glad that you are staying here with me.'

He was staying here, in part, to assume some measure of responsibility for John Thorpe, whose anxiety was not much in evidence, and who was crashing about in the wreckage of the pavilion but would soon be tired of that. Mr Benson the steward, who had been avoiding the scene of Mr Thorpe's activities but was not happy, remarked to James Morland: 'I have been hoping the Colonel might come down before the – before long; but I am afraid that is now unlikely . . .'

The wet weather still kept the remaining members of the party indoors. The servants were subdued; Roland had put away the bowls and was applying what attention he could to Charles's lessons. '. . . Oh, sir, no,' Charles mentioned apologetically, once or twice, 'you have set me that passage for dictation already – only this morning.'

'I am sorry – I am forgetful. What passage shall I set, then?'

Roland was forgetful of much at the moment; checking the calendar one morning he realised that today was his birthday and that he had attained his majority overnight; he did not announce the fact; nor apparently did his mother remember. It was not a suitable time for celebration.

Roland did not at all understand his mother nowadays. Indeed, he never had; but for some time he had been able to think of nothing except his adoration of Miss Tilney, which he must keep from his mother at all costs; she would deride it, and him, and tell him – which he well knew – that he was in no position to think of love or anything so absurd as marriage; his secret brought him nothing but depression and a sense of unworthiness; yet he could not forget that glance of appeal that Miss Tilney had given him in her anguish when she heard of her mother's peril. The hopeless treasuring of that was a distraction, in which he perceived a difference in his mother that he could not examine; sufficient was it that she was quieter and did not pay him much attention.

Later, he blamed himself severely because in his absence of mind he did not pay attention to his mother's attitude to Charles. Charles was his prime duty; it was Charles however at whose cost Roland kept his own secret; this was unforgivable.

So it rained, and Charles made uncorrected mistakes in his Greek verbs, and Mrs Firth asked Mrs Wight whether, in the absence of Miss Tilney, a dressmaker could be found for her poplin gown? Mrs Wight's expression made it clear that such things ought not to be considered at a time like this; but Mrs Firth insisted; she had to keep herself neat and cheerful.

Charles at the dinner table observed into a silence: 'We

do feel the lack of Miss Tilney, do we not; when there is a lady present, company is always more cheerful.'

Hence, of course, Mrs Firth's quest for a dressmaker; had she perhaps been excessively sober and mournful? She owed it to the others to keep up her spirits and theirs. At the time however she made it clear to Charles that his lack of tact amounted to spitefulness. Charles looked puzzled; James Morland said without indignation:

'Charles, apologise to Mrs Firth.'

'I am sorry, ma'am. I did not mean to say that you were not a lady.'

This could hardly mollify her, but James Morland had turned to Roland with some question about the paintings of Giotto.

At times, Mrs Firth reminded herself, all men – even those of James's quality – could be most unfeeling.

Mrs Firth's own feelings were copious and strong, but not as profound as she was wont to suppose. Later, it was thought by many that she had taunted Charles into venturing down the dark passages into the unknown cellars; but she had meant him to do no such thing, nor meant him to do himself any harm, nor much cared whether he did.

Charles on his part had felt no challenge offered him by Mrs Firth, nor been provoked by her mockery. She it was, however, who had compelled him – or rather, this first experience of cruelty had emanated from her; she spoke of 'spitefulness' and behind her manner he sensed the unsuspected evil and hatred in the world that his protected upbringing had not revealed.

His father had said that Charles was afraid of nothing. Nor was he afraid of ghostly abbots, the dark, or hooting old Generals. The fear he must encounter was one quite strange to him: the fear of solitude – of losing his way – of having no one to save him, should he fall or fail – in essence,

94

though his reasoning did not reach as far as this, the fear of being unloved?

A combination of factors – the absence of Miss Tilney, the dull weather, a certain absence of mind in Mr Firth – led to the culmination of Charles's plans. About these he was perfectly composed and reasonable, and he set about his preparations with practical caution. He could lift his left arm, but could not rely on the grip of those fingers; so he purloined a lantern and tied it, with right hand and teeth, to his chest, padding it with a folded kerchief lest it become too hot. He stowed in his pocket a large ball of twine, since those passages underground were, from John Thorpe's descriptions, very much like a labyrinth. (A classical education is never wasted.) Apart from the inner significance of this enterprise, Charles had been very much interested by all he had heard of the crypt and its location. Understandably, he could not comprehend what John Thorpe had at various times said of it; but it seemed to him that the mysterious passage leading to it, past the old well, must fall short of – indeed veer away from – the site of the old chapel as it had now been established, between the bowling green and the stillroom. Or so John Thorpe had most recently established it. About John Thorpe, Charles was not unsympathetic. He could observe that Mr Thorpe was what schoolboys would call 'cocky'; but Charles was no schoolboy, so he was not disposed, as they would be, to smite the man down in his conceit; instead, he felt a desire, mature beyond his years, that poor Mr Thorpe should not be discountenanced nor disappointed. Charles was not yet cynical enough to see the impossibility of this; it gave an added motive to his undertaking, were it needed. Determined as he was, he did not allow himself to hurry. He must go at night, merely so that he would not be missed; he had checked that the door to the billiard room passage and the door into the north cellars, both opening into the quadrangle as they did, were not locked at night. He was well accustomed to the narrow

95

staircase that led down from his room, avoiding the main stairway; when he had waited until surely everyone was asleep, he quietly descended, pausing at the outer door to see that no lights shone at any of the Abbey windows. The rain fell gently; between the clouds as they slowly drifted there was a half moon, but he did not risk lighting his lantern until he was inside the cellar doorway. This caused him some struggle and burnt fingers, but he was undeterred, and drawing a deep breath, stepped forward.

The passage led past several firm and modern doorways and ended in a barred and solid door that must lead to the outer face of the Abbey. Well, that was most strange; he cast to and fro and was reassured to discover a narrow aperture, half blocked with stones, that might well be the route that Mr Thorpe had recommended to a sweep's boy. Charles could barely slide his way through, but when he did, he was struck at once by a difference in the atmosphere. There was a smell of damp – an unevenness in the floor which had only a few rough flag-stones, and in the walls which were partly of brick, with areas of crumbling earth – he was indeed exploring. He looked carefully back to ensure that he would recognise this exit on his return, and ventured on, mindful to lift his left foot, into the darkness. His lantern presently caught the rim of another wide crack in the wall but Charles told it: 'You are *not* the way I came in!' and placed a small group of stones by it, to prevent any mistake. As he proceeded, the passage did bend slowly to the left; must he by now be beyond the outer wall of the Abbey?— No; there was a turning to the half-right, and a draught of air, coming from where he could not guess. It might be coming between the stones that blocked the left-hand passage; they were more than Charles could hope to shift, so necessarily he bore to the right, along a narrower way floored with heaps of rubble.

What he had not foreseen was that down here it would be so cold. The heat of his lantern was no protection from

96

the dank chill that gripped him, tightened his joints and made him shudder. Cautiously, not to stumble on the loose stones, he forced himself on, and came to a length of wooden gutter that crossed a sudden widening of the ground. The recent rain had not yet affected the spring, so that a mere trickle flowed from the old well into the fissure as directed by the Abbey workmen. Charles, ignorant of their labours, was much puzzled; he pursued the trickle until it disappeared under a scattering of boulders, up which he with some difficulty climbed; they shifted under his feet, and he climbed down again – fortunately, since he had been standing directly above the well shaft and the merely perfunctory blocking of it; by tilting himself back, he tried to shine his light upwards, but could see only a roofing of soil and rotted beams; this, then, could not be the crypt.

He was now painfully cold, tired, and when he turned back to retreat – lost? Behind him were two entries to this rough chamber; by which had he come? They were alike – narrow, stony and, of course, dark. It was too late to think of his ball of twine, which in any case would not have been at all long enough to trace the distance he had covered. How great that distance must have been, Charles only now admitted.

He admitted too that he must try to go no further but must seek his way out. The cold rendered him unsteady and doubtless his lantern would not last for many retracings of his steps; did he not choose the right passage from here, he might have no second choice. He stood with his back to the two holes, to calculate and remember how the approach had first appeared to him. Just then, behind him, something moved – there was a rattle of gravel and a scutter of feet. He turned, just in time to see an animal dash across the chamber and vanish into the shadows beyond the beam of his lantern.

An animal, in this place? A cat – a badger? No – larger than that – and black? Charles waited and listened, but there was silence again. At any rate the creature had been no abbot, and for a ghost it was noisy and solid. Nevertheless Charles was increasingly uneasy. Before his wits quite deserted him he must use his powers of observation and inspect both possible ways out. As he bent into the nearer cleft, he saw a whitish object on the ground; it was a bone. It was long and white and quite possibly a relic of an abbot. This was a kind of triumph and certainly a discovery, if of no particular relevance; but it restored some of Charles's sense of purpose. Picking it up – for this would be a tribute to Mr Thorpe – he reasoned too that he could not have missed this object as he entered the chamber – so, the alternative exit must be his.

Just in case – of what? he set the end of his twine under a boulder and let it unreel as he set out. Behind him he heard another rattle of stones and a kind of rattling growl, and this hurried him on, forgetting caution for a moment that undid him. Slipping on the next undulation of rubble, he struggled to his feet without noticing that he had caught his twine round one ankle. Now he fell full length, on to his right side, striking his head on the wall and knocking himself senseless.

He opened his eyes with no recollection of where he was or why; before he did so, he was thinking: So this is what it is like to die. And I am not afraid of it.

It was a reassurance that he had not sought, for it was not death that he had feared. He knew in this moment, however, a serenity that encompassed and exceeded any power of evil or pain that the world could inflict. Charles was afraid of nothing.

This recognition subsided as he became more fully conscious and normality returned, with the admission that he was certainly afraid of the creature whose glittering eyes were fixed on him in the lantern beam. The growl that now echoed along the dank cavern was more alarming than any hooting of a General. And Charles, striving to rise, cried aloud at the agony that gave him; his right arm would not support him, but burnt with pain as if all its bones were shattered. He screamed more shrilly – and the creature of the terrifying eyes moved, as if shrinking back.

A little more normality returned. So it was a dog – as the lantern showed in closeness – but no Xerxes. It was wild and murderous. Yet it had withdrawn when he screamed. Charles with a courageous effort this time began to drag himself to a sitting position, which brought from him another scream, unforced. His arm began to throb and tears poured down his face. The dog had tried to circle him but had not attacked; 'Go away!' screamed Charles, and again it hesitated; there issued another, but more plaintive growl. Could it be, Charles wondered, that it wanted his bone?

'No!' he shouted in what he hoped was a manly and commanding voice. 'You can not have it. Go *away!*' The frustration of his disability was overwhelming – if only he could have thrown stones at it—

The dog flashed its teeth in a hideous grin but, as Charles drew up his feet to try and stand, it backed off. It looked mad enough; Charles told it: 'I will not develop rabies, on top of everything else,' and it gave him one more menacing glare before withdrawing into a shadowed cavity of the passage's side. Charles – remarkably composed considering the dangers – slowly thrust himself upright, his back to the earthern wall, and shouted:

'I suppose, that is my way out, and you are lying in wait for me as I come through!' When he swayed to the aperture and let the lantern beam shine through, there was a flash of teeth and a growl, but he decided: 'If I can stand up, then I could kick it!' and thus armed, faint with pain and cold as he was, he stepped forward – without, as it happened, noticing the pile of stones he had left in just this place, to remind him that this was not the way he had come in.

—But the bone? He must carry it. He remembered the advice one of his doctors had given him, about the weakness of his left hand: 'You must look *hard* at your hand and *will* it to obey you.' But now he tried the same method on his right hand; he willed it to obey him and to pick up the bone; and so it painfully did. 'You see,' Charles adjured his right arm, 'you are not broken. Just do your work. Thank you . . .'

The picking up of the bone had a surprising result: The dog slunk away, with a sound like a whimper, and watched again from a slight distance. 'So,' Charles said, 'it was the bone you wanted? You would not gain much benefit, as Mr Thorpe said, from the bones of long-dead abbots.' At his feet he saw a piece of rag, which he willed his right hand to pick up and wrap round the bone, lest the beast made another attempt to seize it. Then, still faint and shuddering and with his arm more painful after its exertions, he set out in the opposite direction from that taken by the dog, only to come up against a brick wall.

The dog had now disappeared, and Charles, retracing his way patiently, did after a time discover his mistake. He did not yet know that he was mistaken about his precious bone: It was a shin of veal from the Abbey kitchens, perhaps three weeks old. The dog, wild enough, was a bitch who had made her way into the Abbey's secret underworld, bringing her bone with her, in search of a place to whelp. Had Charles known this he might have felt obliged to treat her more civilly, but that might not have been to his advantage.

As it was, he was at a grave disadvantage when he finally emerged from the catacomb on that early morning. His right arm was horribly swollen, he was chilled through and dirty and exhausted, and could barely drag himself up to his room and shrug off his now extinguished lantern before he fell upon the floor in a kind of fever. He had not been missed; his adventures had taken up less time than he thought – indeed he would have said he had been several days away – and he lay on the floor for the remaining hours of the night. It was the housemaid who came in to open his

100

curtains who ran to beat on Roland's door, crying: 'Thieves! Murderers! Master Charles has been attacked—'

When it was recognised that this was not so, the consternation of the household was scarcely less. Charles was put to bed and a doctor summoned; the right arm was pronounced to be not broken, but badly wrenched and bruised; the immediate danger, the doctor pronounced, was of an affection of the lungs as a result of severe chill. No one had time at first to inquire into Charles's adventures nor his motives. He would say only: 'I did not find the crypt but I found a bone.' He smiled; he was apparently in a mild delirium. Charles was, in fact, very happy; for much of the time he dreamt that he was floating on a gently swaying black sea, perfectly at peace.

James Morland said to Roland: 'I cannot believe that he did actually go alone into those cellars. He is not a disobedient boy?'

Roland answered: 'Why should he pretend? And he certainly *looks* as if he did.'

John Thorpe on hearing that Charles had found a bone went instantly up and burst into the sickroom. When he returned he announced: '*This* is his bone – *pah*. It stinks. He says he brought it for me. But he did go down there, the young beggar – I can prove that; he found my kerchief!' Waving the rag that had wrapped the bone, he added: 'The boy is a marvel!'

11

It need not perhaps be said, that to Mrs Firth Charles was in no way marvellous. 'How dare he cause us such an alarm,' she demanded of James Morland, 'when we are already in so much anxiety?' Nothing had yet been heard from London about Mrs Tilney; Mrs Firth was in great suspense over the situation there, but alarm was not what she felt over the condition of Charles. 'He lies there,' she continued, 'with everyone cosseting him – when he brought this illness wholly upon himself by an act of childish mischief. I have no patience with him.'

They were walking in the shrubbery; the rain had cleared, and the gardens of the Abbey sparkled with freshness. Distantly could be heard heavy thuds as of falling stones; was her brother resuming his activity of wrecking this hallowed place? He had stated this morning that he intended to widen the passage into the west corner of the cloister.

'I have observed that,' said James Morland, seriously.

'You have observed what, James?'

'It is rather too clear, Mrs Firth, that you have little patience with Charles.'

She had, also, little patience at this moment with her James, who persisted in addressing her so formally. At one time she had been his 'dear Isabella' but had failed to remind him of that, during all this closer association; with

John busy, and Roland sitting for most of the day with Charles, surely James and Isabella must rediscover their love? She said, in a pettish tone:

'I do not know what you mean by *too* clear. He has never suffered from my manner to him. And, you must admit, he has been badly spoilt. He needs to be taught that he is not the only person in the world.'

'We all need to be reminded of that, I suppose,' said James Morland in a meditative mood. When, earlier, he had visited Charles, he had noticed a change in the boy: It was as if he had had an experience that had driven him deeper into himself and given him a new self-certainty. Of course, the boy was still in a low fever – but, in a sense, it could be beneficial to see the world, sometimes, in relation to one's self? This was not, he knew, what Mrs Firth had implied, and he may have deserved her reply to his platitude:

'James, you speak like a preacher!'

He smiled at her, apologetic. She seemed to forget that so he was. 'We should be thankful that the boy is recovering after his exposure, alarming as it was. I know Roland has been much concerned for him.'

'So he should be; he is responsible for the child.'

Roland was aware of his responsibility and ashamed that he might have failed in it. Charles however was not in the least reproachful; he was sorry to have caused trouble by being ill but appeared in no way to regret his frightening adventure; he had been, in fact, not frightened. His fever had abated but his right arm, swollen even to the fingers, was as useless at present as his left. Roland, and relays of housemaids, had to feed him, vying with each other for the honour. 'I shall soon be able to hold a book,' Charles said after Roland had read him a chapter of Sir Walter Scott, 'but when shall I hold a pen again?'

'I will write to your mother for you—'

'But, please, Mr Firth, do not tell her about my accident!'

103

'Why not? She will worry – but more, if she does not hear from you.'

'There is no reason for her to worry, is there?'

Roland pondered. 'We may tell her that you have hurt your hand – which is no lie; and you can dictate a good cheerful letter to her.'

'But I am good and cheerful,' said Charles laughing, 'so that will be no lie either.'

The letter was dictated and sent, and soon after, as the sun still shone, the doctor permitted Charles to leave his room and sit out of doors. 'What a relief it is,' James Morland remarked to Mrs Firth, 'that he was so quick to recover.'

Mrs Firth had been irritated by the sight of the good and cheerful Charles in the cloister corner, being fed with slices of peach from the wall that her brother threatened before long to demolish. She was becoming a little irritated too by the frequency of James's approving comments on the child. 'I think he should go home. He would be better there, than here among strangers. I wonder his father has not sent for him.'

'He seems perfectly happy here.'

'No wonder, pampered as he is.'

James Morland glanced at her in some disquiet. The tone of his conversations with Mrs Firth had lately deteriorated; she was sharp and inconsequent and inattentive, and he was almost discouraged in his intentions toward her, but reproved himself for that. She must be concerned for Mrs Tilney, of whom they had still heard nothing. 'Your own thoughts, I surmise, and I cannot query that, are much in London.'

'Well, and is it not time they sent us news? Miss Tilney could surely find a moment to write to you – her uncle. Though probably, Colonel Tilney monopolises his daughters' time; he may have had great need of their support, and will for some while after the funeral and its duties.'

'The funeral?' echoed James Morland astonished. 'Why –

What have you heard, that I have not? Can Mrs Tilney have . . . passed away?'

'Have you heard that she has *not?*' returned Mrs Firth, in a tone of disappointment rather than of hope. 'I do not know that anyone recovers from cholera – and she is said to be delicate.' She added to herself, pausing to gaze down the rose garden: 'She *must* have died.'

The significance of that last sentence James Morland did not dare to perceive. The significance of his throwing doubt on the demise of Mrs Tilney was all too clear to Mrs Firth; she saw that, with the sunshine, the beauty of the Abbey and the preacherish conversation of her James, she had had in mind a happier future for herself, as consolation of the widower, mistress of the Abbey, and in the blooming of a romance broken off in Bath over twenty years ago. She had been prepared to wait until Colonel Tilney's mourning was completed and his grief abated; were he not to be a widower, her heart would be irreparably broken.

'We can, then, still hope,' murmured James Morland.

'I suppose so,' said Mrs Firth ungraciously. People did suffer relapses; convalescence could be weakening; it could last for a long time, however. 'I am going indoors,' she announced, turning away. 'I find this sun uncomfortably hot. Good day to you, Mr Morland.'

In London at this time it was uncomfortably hot. Frederick Tilney sat, idle and restless, behind shutters that shaded the room from the intrusive sun, but cut off the sight of the life of the world outside, of the passing carriages and river craft and happy activity of people unplagued by the stuffy air of illness that had held this house in thrall for so long. He had a glass in his hand; a newspaper was thrown down at his feet; his half-closed eyes saw nothing; presently they closed and for a brief time he must have slept; he was disturbed by soft footsteps at the door, but they receded. Someone was for ever tiptoeing about; the whole house was one deathly hush – one dared not speak . . . A sudden thrust of headache roused him – by G—, was he ill too? Had he caught that infernal disease? He roared:

'Annabella!'

The soft footsteps returned. 'It is Paulina, Papa.'

'Either of you – Bring me one of those powders, quickly. I have a head like perdition. They are on the bureau there.'

The girl approached, opening the sachet; Frederick seized it from her and spilled the powder into his half-full wine glass.

'Papa, should it be taken with wine? Should I not bring a glass of water—'

'For all hell's sake, do not try to make an invalid of me!' he shouted. 'I will not be *nursed.*' He swallowed the draught, clapped down the glass and added: 'Bring me my newspaper, will you. There will be nothing worth reading but it will pass the time.'

'It is here,' said Paulina, gathering it up and straightening the folds. Her father's eyes were closed again; she dared not offer to read to him since he would not be treated as an invalid; she laid it on the table beside him. 'May I bring you anything else?'

'Since it does not occur to you to offer to read to me, and spare my eyes – No. Go away.'

Paulina left the room, leaving the door open, as were all the doors in the house, to allow some air to circulate. She went down to the little back parlour where her sister was lying along the window seat reading a novel. She closed the book on one finger and inquired: 'What was all that?'

'It was just Papa—'

'So I could hear.'

Paulina looked upwards, as if studying the renewed silence of the house. 'He wanted a powder – He has the headache.'

Annabella sat up, pushing back from her brow the curls of hair that in spite of the open window were damp. She sighed. 'Of the two, he is giving more trouble than Mama.'

106

This was true, but both young ladies in fact wished that their mother would demand more attention – indeed, that she would be roused to demand anything. Poor Mrs Tilney, wasted and comatose, seemed to be kept barely alive by the skill of doctors and nurses. Paulina murmured: 'But Papa is so much troubled about her – He is not accustomed to illnesses—'

'Well, nor am I,' returned Annabella with an impatience that implied no disregard for her mother, but some understandable selfishness at being trapped in this house of looming death instead of being, as she should be, in Scotland. 'Nor you – It was good of you to come, Polly, and I should have died myself without you. But I suppose we must both stay.'

'Oh, yes. While Papa is so lonely, and feels he must stay at hand—' She had seated herself at the table and taken up some sewing, but just then a roaring from upstairs and the banging of a door made them both glance up. Colonel Tilney's roar was answered by the voice of a man – his valet. Paulina and Annabella looked at each other in query, but did not move; and soon the valet appeared at the door of the parlour to say:

'Colonel Tilney is going to his club for half an hour, Miss Tilney.'

This, the afflicted Colonel had now and then resorted to; the half hour might extend into the evening. The sisters were to be relieved at least of sudden uproar; they smiled at one another. The valet added:

'And the nurse says, if you please, that it is time for Mrs Tilney's linen.'

This meant, that their mother's nightgown or sheets were to be changed, as happened many times in a day. If Mrs Tilney were to be disturbed, for nourishment or washing, the doctor had advised that some member of the family should be present, in case the disturbance should rouse her sufficiently to recognise anyone, which would be a promising sign.

'It is my turn – thank you, Jarvis,' said Annabella, jumping up. This attendance was, naturally, a severe ordeal for the girls and they had agreed to share it. Paulina gave her sister a smile of gratitude, and Annabella on her way to go upstairs whispered: 'If Papa is still out, shall we have fried herrings for supper?'

This was to encourage herself as well as Paulina. Annabella ran lightly up the stairs into the dread sickroom with its fumes of camphor wick and cologne. She stood at the foot of the bed, in line with the gaze of those hollow eyes, should they open. The nurses, deft and gentle, had no exertion in lifting the frail body: the shrivelled and waxen features gave no stir of consciousness. When all was tidy, Annabella came to sit on the side of the bed. As the nurse smoothed a cool cloth over her mother's face Annabella took one of the hot hands in her own and whispered:

'Mama . . . Mama . . .?'

She felt the thin fingers in her own give a slight twitch; then, to Annabella's surprise, the eyelids also quivered. The eyes opened; they did not raise themselves to Annabella's face but appeared to fix darkly on the sash of Annabella's gown as it lay across the bed cover. At this, the nurses stood silent, sharing Annabella's astonishment. 'Mama?' repeated Annabella.

Mrs Tilney's face contracted as if in a frown. Her hand slipped out of Annabella's and wavered towards the sash. She opened her cracked lips to form a word, which she forced herself to say again, with a curious emphasis. The nurses bent to hear. 'What is she saying?' whispered one. 'Is it your name, my dear? Or is it "You"—What is worrying her?'

'I know,' exclaimed Annabella. Mrs Tilney's eyes had closed again and she was no longer conscious. 'She was trying to say "blue" – but she could not make her lips close

– Mama always told me I should not wear this green ribbon with this gown – she said I must wear my blue . . . Oh Mama,' she said, breaking into tears, 'I will change it for my blue, at once—She did notice, did she not?' she appealed to the nurses. 'She *knew*—'

The nurses agreed that Mrs Tilney had shown a most promising degree of awareness. When Annabella had run downstairs to tell Paulina of this wonderful development, the senior nurse who had known Mrs Tilney in previous illnesses remarked to her assistant:

'I must say, this really is a sign of progress. Of course, being Mrs Tilney, when she turned back from the brink of the grave, the first thing she would think about would be clothes. We might say she is becoming herself again.'

12

The promise of recovery had not been delusory; from that first perception of the green sash, Mrs Tilney had gradually lengthening periods of awareness. The household was much relieved.

'As soon as she is well,' said Annabella to Paulina, 'I shall be able to go away—Oh, what a joy that will be! Do you know, all the time we were in France I did not go to a single ball; I had hoped we would go to the Duchesnes, where there would be dancing – but, no, and even at the château I had to stay beside Mama as often as not when they all went out on gay picnics—Well, I did have one moonlight drive with Hortense and her brother, but I declare, for all the pleasure I had, I might as well have been stuck away like you at that boring old Abbey!'

Paulina did not protest at the adjective, although the Abbey and its company were much, and wistfully, in her thoughts. Nor did she warn her sister that their mother might not for a long while be well enough to dispense with their care. She admitted to herself that, were one of the daughters to be released, it should be Annabella. Annabella readily accepted the suggestion.

'Well, and I have been tied down this long time. And I suppose you will do as well here as anywhere – since you do not need society as much as I do. I expect you are glad to be in town again even in this hot weather and subjection. Yes, I may call it that! Do not look disapproval. There will be more callers when Mama is up, and it is time too that you looked for a husband—There cannot be much chance, in Gloucestershire.—Why, Polly, you are blushing—Have I annoyed you? I know I speak too freely—'

'To me, you may speak as you wish; you know that.' Paulina for a moment put her hands to her cheeks as if to hide their treacherous colour. She felt an almost passionate longing for the sunny cloister with Roland and Charles at their books, and Uncle James of course— And how was Mr Thorpe progressing with his chapel? Some one of them might have written to her, but she imagined they believed her absorbed in her family – which she was. She remarked:

'Mama is to sit up for an hour today, the doctor said. Do you notice, the nurses have removed the looking glass from her room?'

'That was wise. I am afraid she may be upset when she sees herself. It is sad, that she is grown so altered.'

The Colonel, whose visits to his wife hitherto had been short and perfunctory, expressed a similar opinion after he had been up to see her raised on her pillows.

'Lord, what a hideous crone she looks!' he complained to his daughters. 'I did not know she was so thin. And what has happened to her hair? There she sits, moaning because they will not show her a glass – I swear, it would kill her outright!' He sounded as if he felt that might be only merciful. Dropping heavily into his chair he asserted scowling:

'So this will be a long convalescence, that fool of a doctor told me. And what am *I* to do with myself while she is in this state? It was very well for me to hang about and attend on her when she was dying – but if she is not, why have I wasted most of the summer when I could have been enjoying myself. I have missed half a dozen race meetings for her – and as it is, most of my friends are still out of town.'

A less dutiful daughter than Paulina might have let herself

111

recognise that, staying here with her parents, she would have two massive cases of self-pity on her hands; but pity her mother and father she sincerely did, as she sincerely wished Annabella to be liberated. Glancing out of the window at the humid haze that blanketed the river she suggested:

'Papa, when Mama is strong enough to be moved, would it not help her to have country air? I could take her down to the Abbey where she might have rest and quiet.'

'Nonsense. She always hated that place. So do I. She can rest here, as much as she must, tie *me* down as it may.'

Paulina had offered her suggestion through no self-interest. And, recollecting Mr Thorpe's activities, she admitted that rest and quiet might not be conspicuous among the Abbey's virtues nowadays.

Mr Thorpe, his assault on the stillroom repelled by Mrs Wight unrelentingly, had been excavating the floor of the passage leading from the north-east corner of the quadrangle, and had satisfied himself that the large stone there was very probably the original step at the doorway of the old chapel. This brought him back to the exact starting-point of his quest, but everyone interested was by now confused enough not to observe that, or generous enough not to point it out.

He had lost interest in the crypt. 'If that vaulted what-did-you-say isn't under the chapel I do not want it. And if it is it should have an entry from the chapel. In any case I believe little chimney-boy was right, and that the passage was off course.'

'What I feel should be done,' James Morland told Mrs Firth, 'is the sealing off – with bricks or boards – of all those mysterious regions. Charles was fortunate – and brave; but there could be future generations of children to be put at risk—'

'I do not see that Charles is specially brave. I am sure that

112

Captain – that is, Colonel – Tilney as a boy would have done better.'

'He, too, has survived such an adventure. But I was thinking of children to come.'

'Whose children would they be?' mused Mrs Firth.

'Do you mean . . . who is to inherit the Abbey? I do not know. I have not heard of any entail, for instance; or whether the property is Colonel Tilney's to bequeath as he chooses; if so, Paulina will inherit; though Henry Tilney has sons—'

'Miss Tilney will need to make a careful choice of husband,' Mrs Firth said with a resentment that James Morland could not account for. But Mrs Firth could not from delicacy – nor from desire – point out that she herself was regrettably past the age of childbearing.

'I am sure she will do that,' James Morland reassured her. It then occurred to him that – as far as he had observed – Paulina had, on these premises at this time, a young man who would make her a charming husband and who had given indications, deliberate or not, of feeling that Paulina would make a charming wife. James wondered that Mrs Firth did not sound more delighted that her own grandchildren might be brought up at the Abbey, dangerous subterranean regions or not. Fortunately he did not say so, but mentioned obliquely:

'The choice of a lifetime's companion is a grave matter. I expect you are watchful over your own son's attachments—'

'Oh, Roland; he is too young to have attachments, and besides, he has no money. I myself have learnt wisdom; my own first choice was disastrous; I shall not, a second time, act with so little foresight.'

'I hope your choice will be . . . rewarded.' He felt that this was the moment for him to offer himself to her choice; but like a coward he delayed it. Or was it, he then wondered, that she did not mean to give him the opportunity? He could not deny that her manner towards him had become a great deal cooler – nay, unfriendly – of late. He could

113

not guess how he had failed her; she had at first been so approachable – almost affectionate; now, it was not only that she spoke as if she did not at all care for him – which he had not been conceited enough to expect – but that her attitude in so many things – in her treatment of Charles, her indifference to the wellbeing of Roland or the convenience of the servants – all bespoke the frivolity that he had pitied; James, that professed saviour of sinners, had not succeeded here, great as was the sacrifice he had been prepared to make for her.

His sense of failure made him more solemn than usual. He did not await any reply to his courteous hope, but after a pause Mrs Firth said:

'I thank you. I am hopeful myself that it will. I may have to be patient . . . for a short time.'

James Morland did not know what to make of that. Could it mean that she had some second choice – a prospective second husband – in view? Far from feeling rejected or excluded he felt marvellously relieved for an instant, before he could check that unworthy impulse. He changed the subject:

'I wonder that we have still no news from London. It is strange.'

'It will come. There must be much sadness there.'

'I thought of sending to Woodston, in case they know more?'

Mrs Firth said: 'Oh, I think you need not to interfere in the affairs of the Tilney family.'

The two of them, as they reached the top of the shrubbery path, paused; a breeze swept across the lawns and Mrs ~~Tilney~~ Firth pulled her lace shawl closer round her throat. As she did so she accidentally tore loose the chain that held a cross set with seed pearls that she wore on her gown; James stooped to pick it up for her.

'This is a handsome piece of work,' he said as he handed it to her.

114

'It is only a trinket,' said Mrs Firth, impatiently dropping it into her carrying bag. 'It grows chilly; I shall go back to the house. Why do you yourself not go to Woodston? I understood that you were a guest there, and came to the Abbey only as company for Miss Tilney.'

'That is true. I had not intended to be so long away from my sister's. I hoped, I confess, to be of some use – to bear some company – by staying here.'

He said this very humbly, gazing earnestly at her, but Mrs Firth was already turning to walk away. Over her shoulder she said, shivering a little in the breeze: 'I do not know of what use you have been, and nor have you been the most lively company, with your preachings and gloomy warnings. By all means, go back to your sister's and shed your gloom on her.'

James's gloom deepened into depression as he accepted his dismissal. He had suppressed his previous impulse of relief and encountered the full abjectness of his failure with her.

Next morning he departed for Woodston; Roland and Charles deplored his going and hoped to see him again very soon; Charles gave him a present of a silver pen knife, a legacy from his own grandfather. Neither John Thorpe nor Mrs Firth was at hand to join in the farewells.

Roland missed Mr Morland. He had found that gentleman a comforting avuncular presence – and had been grateful that he had befriended Roland's mother, which had been as Roland saw it greatly to his mother's advantage. With Mr Morland she had behaved with a dignity and amiability suitable to a mother; not that Roland would so have described it, nor did he suspect Mrs Firth's designs on Mr Morland. Had he been apprised of these, he would have welcomed Mr Morland as stepfather.

Since the terrible news of Mrs Tinley's illness, Roland had had to observe that the manner of both his mother and of

Mr Morland had, not surprisingly, altered; it was to this only that Roland ascribed the increasing gravity of Mr Morland and the increasing restlessness of Mrs Firth. Now that Mrs Firth was more alone, she had leisure to find fault with everyone; John Thorpe was too indolent yet in too much haste to make a wreckage of the Abbey; Roland was unhelpful yet spent his time on Charles, fussing over the boy; Charles was acting the invalid yet becoming too impertinent and boastful; and the dressmaker summoned by Mrs Wight was rendering Mrs Firth's new gown as plain and commonplace as if it were for a parson's wife. The servants were all careless and out of hand. And who, she demanded, had ordered a fire lit in the drawing room, with the sun shining as it was?

Roland told her: 'The wind is cold; do you not find it so? When the doctor came, he said that Charles must be kept quite warm. He is not yet satisfied that the chill is warded off.'

'I hardly suppose the doctor need still be calling; Charles looks in perfect health, and you never cease to bandage and salve him. That bruise on his face will heal itself. I hope it soon will; it makes him look a fright. But there is no company here to see him.'

The contusion to Charles's face when his head struck the wall of the underground passage was by now in its stage of radiant colour, passing from blue to green and purple; he gave Mrs Firth his lop-sided and lurid smile and agreed that he did indeed look unattractive. 'But my mother often says I lack colour in my face—She for one might be pleased.'

'It is nothing to make a joke of,' Mrs Firth reproved him.

Roland admired Charles for his levity and applied himself willingly to renewing the compresses on the bruised arm and to keeping Charles warm and happy. Rather, it was Charles who alone kept Roland happy, or as happy as the absence of Miss Tilney could make him. Charles remained as cheerful as he had been since his adventure; Roland

116

wondered whether this might be some form of nervous reaction, and whether he should not remonstrate mildly:

'But you realise, do you not, that it was both dangerous and disobedient, to go exploring like that?'

'Yes and I am sorry, but it was not you whom I disobeyed. No, I did disobey – and I did not achieve anything except a piece of kitchen bone. What I mean is that I disobeyed some rules that turned out to be not important.'

'All rules are important,' said his tutor sententiously.

'Until you break them,' added Charles with a precocity that Mrs Firth would have despised. 'You see – I have always known that I was not like other people – in my awkwardness and shape – and I thought there was a sort of rule: All boys should be agile and love games and go to school; and if I did not keep to that, I must try to copy it.' He frowned. '— Or I must be sorry I was not like it. Well, when I was still lying in bed, and Mr Morland came to visit me, he read some prayers for me, and told me very seriously about the ways of God and how we ought to follow them even if we did not see why at first. So then, I thought: Is it the way of God that boys must go to school and have strong legs and climb trees? So then, I thought: No. God has broken that rule.'

Mrs Firth would have thrown up her hands in horror at this blasphemy but Roland understood despite the fumbling words. He said: 'Indeed, God wants you to find your *own* way.'

'Yes, I suppose that is what I mean. I did not tell Mr Morland what I thought. He is so serious. But I am sorry he is gone.'

'So am I. He could have taught you much—'

'Not as much as you can,' said Charles, as sincere as tactful.

'Besides, I am sure you can teach me more than I would learn at a school. Have I not worked well, and progressed fast, since we came here? Do you know what I would like:

117

To stay here with you – and Miss Tilney – and Xerxes, and Mr Thorpe and his plans, until I go to university?'

'You intend to go to university, then?' said Roland smiling to cover the shock of Miss Tilney's name.

'Oh yes. I think that is one of my rules. By then, I shall have grown taller and my left leg will be quite strong. Of course I shall want to be with Mama and Papa too . . .' he added; but his tact did not reach to the extent of mentioning Mrs Firth.

Mrs Firth was half apologetic that her dear James had gone away so doleful; but he should have known what to expect, with Frederick Tilney in prospect. She was amused to recollect that the history of over twenty years ago was repeating itself: Then she had been engaged to marry James, but as soon as handsome Captain Tilney invited her to dance, James became so jealous that he withdrew; nor could he have the courtesy to renew his attentions to young Isabella when she discarded Captain Tilney as too frivolous; that James should still be a victim of jealousy befitted neither his mature years nor his cloth.

Captain – Colonel – Tilney on the other hand would have advanced in maturity as he had in rank. She was impatient to see him but patient enough to wait before seeking a way of bringing this about: if she had not to wait too long.

When Roland had escorted Charles to bed (as if every housemaid in the place would not be eager to perform that office) she settled herself comfortably with a novel beside the drawing room fire, glad of a little peace. But soon her brother burst out of the breakfast room and came stamping across the hall.

'Ho there! Still disporting yourself like the lady of the manor? You could not stir yourself to help me by making a fresh copy of my plan of the chapel? Young Sweep cannot yet use that hand, and I have spilt wine on this.'

'I cannot be responsible for your drinking habits nor your inefficiency.'

'I admit neither. Give me a clean sheet of paper and I will do it myself – but it will take time that I cannot spare.'

'John, listen to me. You have spared so much time over your plans and foolery that I begin to doubt you will accomplish anything at all.'

'I never yet failed in any objective I set myself to,' proclaimed John Thorpe in a bluster; his sister did not trouble to contradict, but went on:

'It is to be hoped that you can tidy up your work, at least, in case the Colonel should come down—'

'Why the deuce should he come down? He never does.'

'His circumstances have altered, as you know.'

'Well if they have, mine have not. And it was he who sent me here; he cannot complain.'

'But, as you mention that, should Roland and that boy be here if Colonel Tilney arrives and wants peace at the Abbey? They were not invited by him.'

'Were *you?*' retaliated John Thorpe.

His sister merely allowed herself a faint smile. It remained to be seen what her status at the Abbey was to be.

119

13

The same cooler wind was blowing over Birmingham. It brought no relief to the men who toiled at the furnaces of Jacob Ballard's foundries, but it swirled fumes and grit up to the windows of his house. 'Young Charles is well away from this,' observed Jacob Ballard, running his finger along a sill.

'But,' implored Mrs Ballard, as she had implored for so long, since Charles's cheerfully dictated letter, 'he can not be safe in that place in Gloucestershire. How could they let him fall? What can Mr Firth have been thinking of? I have been used to believe him so careful. His right hand, too – the poor child, his one good hand! He should be brought home, where he has been used to smuts on the windowsills for all his life. He must be completely *helpless*—'

'Not he,' said Mr Ballard.

The same wind brought dust and odours to the house of the Tilneys, but it ruffled the river and scattered its mists, and brought some relief to Mrs Tilney. Once she was able to sit up and take more nourishment, her recovery gathered impetus. This in turn was accelerated by her dissatisfaction with the world and herself – more especially when the looking glass was reluctantly shown to her.

'I wish I had died!' she exclaimed several times in a day,

as her daughters applied salves and lotions to her sunken cheeks and gently tended the scanty locks of her hair. 'Annabella, that is doing no good – I can feel it shrinking my skin – Try some rosewater – Paulina, do not pull so hard—Stop, stop! You will pull what hair I have *out*, instead of stimulating its growth—' And there came a day whereon she cried: 'Give me the comb—' and, when her weakened claw of a hand could not wield the comb, she dropped it and wept. 'Oh, I wish I had died! Go away, both of you – you will just come to hate me because I am so ugly – I hate you both!'

They were patient; they were unhappy. It was Mrs Grant, their old nurse, who consoled them:

'Do you not see, my dears, that what she hates is your lovely and healthy young faces in contrast to hers; let me go to her.'

Mrs Grant was healthy, but could gracefully admit that she was neither lovely nor young; so it was she, along with the senior nurse, who assumed the routine of beautifying. They had no more apparent success, naturally – only time and nature might do that – but Mrs Tilney tolerated their treatments with much lamenting but less anger. To Paulina and Annabella were left such tasks as reading aloud, arranging flowers and planning tempting little meals. In addition they still had to minister to their father, whose beauty they did not aspire to restore and whose temper they could but suffer.

'So your mother is supposed to be better,' he grumbled, 'yet she looks more scrawny than ever – and does nothing but complain. It is nothing to her that I have been tied to the house for all these weeks on end—Is it my fault that she was afflicted with this disgusting disease? She should think of me and be thankful that I was not infected too.'

'We are thankful for that, Papa,' said Annabella.

'Is that an impudent smile on your face, Miss? I'll thank you to wipe it off. Bring me my tobacco jar.'

Annabella said later to Paulina: 'I did not mean to be impudent to Papa; why should he think so?'

Paulina could believe that Annabella had not meant to provoke more of her father's wrath than was often visited upon his daughters nowadays, and for which there was rarely a specific reason. Such constant buffeting was however taking effect on Annabella's own nerves; when Paulina mentioned that their father had been through a great deal of anxiety, it was in a pettish tone that Annabella retorted:

'Well, so have we all. I do not see that he needs to bellow at us so much. And he has not been for weeks in the house— He has, I suppose, but he often goes to his club. And he is drinking too much.'

At this last, Paulina checked the tirade with a glance of reproof and horror. Dropping her own eyes Annabella continued: 'Oh, I am sorry – I did not mean . . .' Since she could not in honesty retract what she had said, she went on: 'And what shall we do about Edwards?'

Edwards was Mrs Tilney's personal maid, skilled in arranging her mistress's elaborate curls and ball gowns; two days ago she must have made some sympathetic reference to these lost glories, whereat Mrs Tilney had immediately dismissed her. The household agreed that Mrs Tilney would regret this, and Paulina and Annabella had applied to their father: Could Edwards be sent away only temporarily – given, perhaps a form of holiday? The Colonel had flown into a fury, demanding to know what was wrong with the world when servants could be sent on holiday from a hard-pressed staff; he sent for the housekeeper and commanded her to have that stupid woman out of the house within an hour, a command which was necessarily obeyed. Paulina said now:

'Nana has sent to find out, and Edwards has gone to her sister's in Bermondsey, as she said she would. I told Nana that one of us should go to see her, but Nana thought Papa would be angry, if he asked where we had been—'

'He would blaze with rage!' cried Annabella with a dramatic rolling of her eyes. It did not of course occur to either of these young ladies that they might lie to their father, did he inquire into their comings and goings. 'He would throw us out of the house, as he did Edwards—And now I think of it, for my part I should be pleased if he did.'

Paulina, sighing, thrust her needle vigorously into her work. In a repressive voice she said: 'Nana said that she herself would go, perhaps taking one of the footmen. It may well be that Edwards has not yet sought another position, and we could offer her a fee, for a while, lest she do so.'

'If she has not taken offence—'

'But, you know, she was devoted to Mama.'

'Was,' echoed Annabella with significance. She too sighed. 'Very well then; you and Nana arrange it all, between you. I find all these rages and squabbles so tedious . . .'

Annabella was not alone in that. 'I will write a note to Edwards, that Nana can take to her. Do you not think, Belle, that if you chose your moment, you could ask Papa whether you might go to the Harringtons – just for a short visit?'

Annabella laughed, scornful. 'Could I expect a holiday, when the servants are not permitted them?' She was attracted however by the suggestion. 'I believe they are back at home now, in Cromer. Oh, for sea air! I wish Mrs Harrington might fall ill, then I could have an excuse to go.—No, do not look so shocked; you are always disapproving of me nowadays. I do seriously long to see Jane and Maria.'

From this conversation, Paulina concluded that a change of scene must be provided for Annabella – the more so, if Annabella was becoming irritated by her sister. Paulina saw herself at present as dull and prim as Annabella seemed to; squabbles could not be allowed to pervade the whole house. She tried to think of a way of persuading her father to let Annabella free, but was forestalled by Annabella herself who, if not so thoughtful as her elder sister, was better endowed with natural cunning. Annabella, choosing a moment that might not have appeared suitable, appealed to her mother;

Mrs Tilney, just then distraught over her doctor's advice that she wear eyeglasses, cried: 'Oh, yes, go away—Go where you will, and be young and happy—Forget me! I never want to see you again!'

Placing a modified interpretation on this, Annabella chose to intercept her father as he was leaving the house on the way to his club. Hanging on his arm as the servant held open the door she begged: 'Papa—Please wait – Mama wants me to go away, but I will not, if you cannot spare me? I could go to the Harringtons for a while— They would have me; but I am sure you would rather I stayed?'

'Why should I care? I see why your mother wants rid of you – squealing and complaining—Let go of my coat. I have had enough of women shrieking about the house. Let us for G—'s sake have a bit of peace.'

It was true that since Mrs Tilney's condition began to mend, the house had not been in its fraught silence; there was bellowing, banging of doors, wails from Mrs Tilney and the scuttling up and down of servants. When Annabella had gone, beaming and pretty as a nosegay in her best summer dress, no one seemed to miss her; Paulina now took refuge in the old nursery, where she had long and comfortable conversations with Mrs Grant. Paulina herself did not observe how often these conversations turned to the Abbey.

Mrs Grant had often been there in the past, taking her little charges on their summer visits to the frightening grandfather. Since the General's death, she had heard that Paulina had been there from Woodston; while Mrs Grant recalled with amusement incidents from the earlier time, such as the tree-house in the yew hedge, she found that Paulina, also amused, still tended to speak of the Abbey as it was now – and had been, until she left it in such sad circumstances not long ago.

On that day, Mrs Grant had understandably been taken up by her mission and had paid little attention to the persons she had met, nor the improvements being wrought, which were in any case not visible from the front of the building. She shared Paulina's misgivings about the scale of the operations although she agreed that to rebuild the old chapel would be an interesting and beneficial work.

'I am glad your father has undertaken it; it shows that he is, for all he says, fond of the Abbey. But, you feel the plan is not making quick progress?'

'That, so far, is an understatement. Mr Firth points out that more is being dug up, than built. I do wonder what has been done by now,' added Paulina, wistfully.

'Then perhaps, while you have been away, Mr Firth has come to the building stage?'

'Oh – It is not Mr Firth who is building! That is only a remark he made. It is Mr Thorpe – you did not see him; we rarely did – who is the brain behind the scheme.'

'I see. So Mr Firth is the husband of the lady – Mrs Firth – whom I met?'

'No, no – He is her son.'

This puzzled Mrs Grant. 'Nor is he the clergyman who was with her? In fact I felt I had met him—'

'I expect you have; he must have been at Woodston, when we were there as children; but he has grown a beard,' said Paulina, rapidly. 'Uncle James. Aunt Catherine's brother.'

'So who,' pursued Mrs Grant, to set it all straight, 'is that young man with the blue eyes, who was so concerned for you?'

'That is Mr Firth,' said Paulina in a final tone, reaching for her scissors and chopping off her thread. After a moment she asked in an uncertain, studiedly casual tone:

'Did you think him concerned for me?'

Mrs Grant had; even in the emotions of that moment, her protective eye had witnessed and approved the young man's feeling. As casual herself, she merely said: 'Yes; so it seemed to me.'

She checked her curiosity out of regard for Paulina's evident sensitivity but told herself: There was some reason, then, why Paulina is so regretful to be away from the Abbey. I hope she will be able to speak to me about it.

Fond as she was of both her young ladies she allowed herself to reflect: So it may be that Paulina, the country-lover who likes to hide away in Gloucestershire, will find a husband before Annabella, for all that little flirt's attempts.

—But they are both dear good girls, and deserve happiness, after all they have been through with those parents.

The blue-eyed Roland was pleased by the swiftness of Charles's healing: the bruising of his right arm had faded, and the right hand could accomplish a fairly literate rendering of another cheerful letter to Mrs Ballard. 'But, do you know, Mr Firth,' said Charles one sunny morning, 'I have been having a bad dream.'

'About being lost in those dark tunnels?'

'No—Well, yes, but it is about that dog. You said that Mr Morland wanted to see all the entrances to the tunnels sealed up. What if they do seal them up, soon, and the dog should be sealed up inside?'

'I see no work of that sort being begun. And I expect the dog has found his way out long ago – by the same way that he found to get in.'

'I wish I could be sure.'

'May I point out, that there is no question of your going down to ascertain that.'

'No, I know. —Do you suppose Mr Thorpe could find his way down again and just search a little?'

'No. Now please turn to page seventeen, and construe.'

'Yes sir.—But perhaps I will just ask Mr Thorpe what he thinks.'

'If that will stop your bad dream, do. Begin at the first line—'

Roland did not imagine that John Thorpe would be any better acquainted with the underground tunnellings that hitherto, or that he would be interested in stray dogs. What

Roland had not taken into account was John Thorpe's willingness to accept a challenge and his readiness to be distracted by any fresh project. At first he, like Roland, presumed that the dog would have found its way out again; it was only when Charles remarked, half-convinced:

'I took away his bone—But I think, you know, he must have been finding food down there – because he was the fattest dog you ever saw—' that John Thorpe took him up:

'When did you ever see a fat stray dog? It was dark too—'

'My lantern showed it quite clearly. It was very savage-looking but when it turned to go away it *waddled*.'

'Did it. Did she. Was it a bitch?'

Charles stared ignorance, and John explained: 'If he was a she-dog, about to have pups, that might account for it— Otherwise I'd have thought you dreamt it.'

'Pups!' cried Charles, paling. 'Will she have had them yet? Will they be safe, down there? Will they be grown enough to walk—Can they get out? No wonder it was a bad dream—'

'Oh, rubbish. Just as well, if the whole litter was lost. They cannot have been beasts of any value. Come, do not wax sentimental on us. Who is going to chase about in those miles of passages hunting for a savage bitch that will not even be there!' declared John while at the same time his inner voice told him: I am. The fervour of a hunt was upon him.

He rallied his forces. He sent for yards of twine, dozens of lanterns, and for every terrier on the adjoining farms. Almost every man also volunteered; this promised to be an enjoyable affair providing light relief from work. 'Now,' John announced, 'we will tie a length of twine to every terrier and set them into every opening, and have men as back-up to each one – and set lanterns at every turning; we shall have the whole place tooth-combed – and take heavy sticks, in case that brute is still there and fighting.'

'What are the terriers to search for?' asked a boy from the rear of the assembly.

127

'Why – the bitch; will they not? I wish we still had that veal bone – Lord knows it smelt strong; and it must have laid its scent on the bitch. —Wait; I may have the best thing'—He made for the breakfast room, where he had somewhere flung down the kerchief in which Charles had wrapped his unhistorical trophy. John Thorpe was not meticulous in seeing to his own laundry; nor were the servants too conscientious now in dealing with the confusion in the breakfast room, to which the kerchief had been adding its perfume in a strength that no terrier could fail to identify. Returning with the kerchief John thrust it under the nose of all the dogs – who perceptibly recoiled – in turn, hallooing: 'Seek, boy! Seek!'

With yapping and enthusiasm from terriers and men, the entire concourse vanished underground. Roland and Charles waited with trepidation and some disgust, neither knowing whether they wished anything to be found or not; but neither daring to withdraw.

With yellings and flashes of light, with thwacking of sticks, men tripping over twine, laughter and whistles, oaths as men collided with boulders or with each other, the noise was enough to frighten away more than dogs; two men fell into a fist-fight over a dropped lantern, and a local reprobate, a tinker named Zebedee, somehow found his way into the Abbey wine cellars; but the uproar delighted everyone; most of the hunters began to stumble to and fro with no heed for their quarry, exulting in a game of buffet-and-run, huzzas and guffaws echoing round and round again.

Three, in all the tumult, preserved their dignity: Willy, son of Tom the stonemason, who had brought his own terrier and wished to train the dog seriously; the bitch, who knew herself outfaced, so early made her way out by the way she had entered; and her surviving pup, who stood, unsteady but alive, beside the bodies of his six dead siblings, blinking into the first light he had yet seen in his short life.

Among the few dedicated followers, a silence fell. One of

them had carried a sack, into which he gathered the six little bodies; Willy pointed his terrier, feeling the pup's mother could not be far away, coaxing the terrier to seek; which the terrier did, scuffing his way over some loose rubble and yapping his way into the dark; Willy and his lantern followed, and Tom called: 'Wait, lad—', imagining that the bitch could be strong enough to turn on her pursuers. The way narrowed; 'Bring a spade here!' Tom shouted; heedless of where they might by now be, two of the men dug; the terrier trembled with excitement. John Thorpe, who had been shouting disregarded orders until he was hoarse, approached, and crawled through the rubble to find, as lanterns flashed up and down, that there was some kind of a ceiling above—'The crypt!' he yelled. 'This is your crypt again, is it not, Tom?'

Tom was ahead, using the spade on the mound of rubble and saying: 'Here she got through—See, but maybe she were too heavy with pup to get out after a while—See, now?' With a powerful jab of his spade he let in a diffused daylight; as the others climbed after him, out into the fresh air through a tangle of ash saplings and nettles, and emerged panting into the angle of a broken wall, someone cried:

'Look where we are! She'm well away, that bitch. We'm in the north field below the bowling green and we came out of the old ice-house!'

Someone else climbing out agreed. 'Ay, I remember, do you know—Before the old General had it shifted—Oh, it'll be fifty year ago!'

So that was the explanation of the crypt, as it had been supposed to be. John Thorpe did not hesitate to claim that he himself had solved the mystery.

The bitch was never seen again. Willy took home the surviving pup and cherished it. It grew as strong as its original survival had promised, and into such a splendid dog that its sire was credibly supposed to be one of Lord Alexander's champion foxhounds from the other side of the valley.

At the time Charles after a silent struggle pronounced: 'Of course Willy must have the puppy. He saved it.' And he settled down to pen a tottery but cheerful letter to his mother, telling her of the rescue of the pup without revealing that he himself had any acquaintance with the caverns in which it had occurred.

14

'Papa,' began Paulina with an air of resolution, 'would you like me to write some letters for you?'

'Letters? I cannot cope with such things, in my state. And to whom would you write?'

'There must be many friends who do not yet know how well Mama is recovering. Uncle Henry at Woodston, and the people at the Abbey—'

'I have no friends; they desert anyone who is in trouble. And there are only servants at the Abbey.'

'But perhaps we should write to them – and to Uncle James.'

'Uncle who? Be a good girl and stop worrying me. Write what you please!' He emptied his glass and shut his eyes.

'Thank you. I will show you what I write, of course.' She added as she turned to go: 'I expect you would like to hear about Mr Thorpe, and the progress of his work?'

'I never heard of Mr Thorpe or his work. Ring the bell, will you; my bottle is finished.'

Paulina had turned back. After hesitation she said with a quiet urgency: 'Papa. Forgive me, but I think you must remember Mr Thorpe. John Thorpe. We have known him at Bath. He is a fairly short man, dark, with—'

'M'yes: a cadging little braggart and a liar.' His eyes half opened and glared towards her. 'You have not been having anything to do with such a character?'

'He is at the Abbey. He is planning to rebuild the chapel—'

'A likely tale. There *is* no chapel. Have you rung the bell?'

'In a moment . . . Do you mean that you did not ask him to do that?'

'Ring it *now*, if you please. What are you talking about? How can that fool Thorpe build chapels?'

Paulina had been beginning to wonder, but she said calmly: 'I have been there, Papa. I have seen the work started. I think I must tell you about it, in case you did not yourself give him the order—'

The Colonel's somnolence exploded into rage. He hoisted himself up in his chair shouting: 'Give him the order! Are you out of your mind? Do you mean to tell me that John Thorpe is practising his ignorance of building on *my* Abbey?'

'The work was barely started—'

'And it will d— soon be finished and so will he. Why did you not tell me of this outrage? You are as much to blame!'

Paulina made no excuses. She said: 'I will write, and—'

'You will do nothing of the sort. You have done harm enough already by keeping this from me. I forbid you to warn the knave in any way—You will write to no one, d'you hear me? I shall go down myself – as soon as I feel better – and your mother is stronger – and catch him at his tricks. I shall see him thrashed – and in prison.'

From such a confrontation Paulina would gladly be absent. She said faintly: 'Yes, Papa' and was leaving the room when the Colonel bellowed:

'And you can come with me, what is more, so that I can see how much truth you have told me—You must have been behind the plot yourself, to have been so secretive—Why has heaven cursed me with such a daughter? Now ring that *bell* and *go*!'

Paulina, in extreme trepidation, obeyed; she could almost have hoped at this juncture that her father would not for some time feel better; but in that case would the work on the chapel have progressed even more destructively? For the first time in her life she dreaded the idea of going to the Abbey.

Jacob Ballard very much disliked travelling. He felt like himself only at home, where everything was under his eye. He had no interest in scenery or strange places, and travel was itself so slow and tiresome, with uncomfortable inns, baiting of horses, rough and dirty roads and the general waste of time. On this occasion he had to make it all more tiresome for himself by bringing a dog in the carriage.

Why, asked Mrs Ballard, must he take Xerxes, when he was to bring Charles home directly? Her husband said: 'I have found the dog's whining after Charles as wearing as yours, during the last several weeks.'

The dog enjoyed his ride exuberantly, leaping about in the carriage till Jacob was driven to acquiring a basket and shutting him in that; then the dog barked peevishly till he had to be released; he settled in the end on the box, in the arms of the second coachman, but Jacob was unsettled by that – he was almost jealous. Now and then the servant would call: 'Sir, I think Xerxes could do with a run—' and the whole carriage would have to wait while the servant ran up and down a field with the dog gambolling beside him.

So it was that when the coachman called: 'There is the Abbey now, sir, on the rise ahead—' Jacob, stiff from inactivity, bade the carriage stop, and leaned from the window to study the prospect. Climbing down he announced:

'I would like a short walk. Do you see this path that leads to a gate in the wall? If I turn to the right, I expect I will come to the main gates. Do you drive on, and meet me there, and I will take the dog.'

The Abbey, as seen from this aspect, was larger than Jacob

133

had supposed it. The sun of early evening glinted on its pale stone and pointed windows. The path led beside a field of what must be barley, though Jacob had not seen it before in its unreaped state; should they now be harvesting it, Jacob queried? It had tawny glints in the low sun. Into the rustling stalks Xerxes – who had accompanied Jacob after a surreptitious kick from the second coachman – disappeared, to reappear in pursuit of a rabbit as startled as were dog and man – and dog and rabbit raced ahead to vanish again into the corn. Jacob, arriving a little breathless at the gate in the wall, perceived that he must enter the Abbey grounds here if he wished to reach the main entrance; the terrain to his right had become too rough and overgrown for his townsman's boots. He paused leaning on the gate to look back at the landscape and again at the Abbey; he recollected his promise to his wife, that he would acquire a country estate; he regretted it; what would one find to do with one's time, in all this emptiness? A shout roused him:

'Is this your dog?'

Jacob turned to see the spaniel frolicking round a man who stood at some distance under the Abbey wall. Jacob had forgotten the dog, and approached apologetic:

'He was chasing a rabbit – I am afraid I am on your ground. I do not know how he came here—'

'Leapt the wall. I did not see whether the rabbit did. Where are you bound for?'

'I am visiting the Abbey,' said Jacob, wondering what this man was about; he held a long measuring rod and a spade lay at his feet, but his dress, dishevelled as it was, was not that of a labourer. 'Am I perhaps addressing Colonel Tilney?' Jacob was not yet sure of the terms on which his son and tutor were residing at the Abbey, nor under whose auspices.

'The Colonel is away; I expect I will do. Will you please to hold the end of this rod for a moment . . . D—, I made it four inches just now . . . This business is pressing, I assure you.' He made a scribble in a notebook from his pocket. 'Now, what was it you wanted?'

'My name is Ballard. I believe my son is here—'

'The father of our little chimney sweep!' exclaimed John Thorpe. 'Gad, what an amazing boy he is. You must not mind his purple and yellow face – it will pass. How he goes skipping about on that half-a-leg, and goes crawling for miles under the ground by himself, and fighting off crazy dogs – when he had knocked himself out—Yet he can read Greek, and stand up against my bully of a sister—He's a shrimp of a thing but on my oath, he's afraid of nothing!'

This spontaneous testimonial to his son alarmed Jacob as much as it pleased him. John Thorpe, sincere even when he was exaggerating, was sincere in praising Charles and had no intention of ingratiating himself with Charles's father, who indeed was regarding him with a ferocious frown.

'Crazy dogs . . . chimneys – under the ground . . . What are you telling me?' Jacob demanded.

'Oh, he will tell you; he makes little of it all,' said John Thorpe shrugging. He glanced at Charles's father's face and added: 'I do not say that he might not be afraid of *you*.'

Xerxes, tired of this delay, went into the Abbey in search perhaps of a kitchen and titbits. When he scented Charles there was whining and squealing until they were reunited; Charles was ready to believe that Xerxes had found his way from Birmingham all on his own. The appearance of his father, also on foot and with a severe countenance, was for that reason a little disappointing as well as surprising.

Jacob Ballard had promised Charles's mother that he would bring him home with the proviso: 'If I see fit.' Jacob was wont to use promises to pacify his wife because the woman was so continually begging and pleading. The plan had been that Jacob would call at the Abbey and see how Charles did, then bid him pack his boxes; Jacob would spend the night at an inn and return to collect Charles next morning.

The plan went awry, in part through Jacob's fault; he arrived dustily by a side door – that short walk up the fields had tired him – and received a very pleasant welcome from a lady whom he assumed to be the Colonel's wife? The lady lowered her voice to tell him:

'No, sir. I am afraid Colonel Tilney was bereaved of his wife recently. That is why he is detained in London.'

'No one told me! So it is you who acts as hostess here— My regrets, about Mrs Tilney.'

No one had as yet told the inmates of the Abbey, for that matter, of Mrs Tilney's demise. Mrs Firth was willing to practise as lady of the Abbey; she found Charles's father a not unhandsome man, if a little abrupt in his speech. She told him:

'You must stay with us for a few days at least. We have no chance of much company. I will tell the housekeeper to prepare a room.'

Mrs Wight prepared the room vacated by Mr Morland; the staff was growing accustomed to visitors; it was she who asked Brook the butler how Master Charles's father could have journeyed here?—And it was Brook who espied the carriage waiting by the front gates, and who sent to invite it in, and to retrieve the second coachman who was still running to and fro in search of Mr Ballard.

When he understood that his hostess was the mother of young Firth the tutor, Jacob wondered again at her status here; but the complications of the place did not bother him. Firth was looking well – not so pale and bookish; country air must suit him. He said, tentatively, to Jacob: 'I hope, sir, you do not feel I have failed in my care of Charles.'

'Failed? How?' He contemplated his son who was sprawling on a sofa with the dog. He could see that Charles had had heavy bruises to his face but they were not as vivid as he had been informed; the right hand that could scarcely

guide a pen was fully active in fussing over the beast. That
the dog had taken precedence over the father in Charles's
welcome, persuaded Jacob that the boy was in high natural
spirits. 'Charles is all right. I met an extraordinary fellow on
my way here, who made me hold his measuring rod, and
told me how these misadventures came about . . .' He went
on to describe John Thorpe and young Firth mentioned:
'That was my uncle, sir.'

Added complications, Jacob thought, impatiently. 'You
must tell me what the boy was up to. He seemed to think I
had powers of divination when I said I knew about the
mischief he had been up to. Well, and I shall ask him again
when he leaves off making himself silly like a lady with a
lapdog.—What was this about climbing chimneys?'

Roland said: 'Sometimes, sir, my uncle indulges in . . .
overstatement.'

'Well I am glad to know that.—Wait, Firth; I have a
message for you—Where did I put it—It was in my wallet,
and my wallet was—Where did I leave my carriage?'

That he could forget such a sizeable item as a carriage
helped to suggest to Jacob Ballard that a couple of days of
rest in the country might restore him to his normal state
of efficiency. He forgot too that he had a letter for Roland
Firth and Roland, after a moment's wild hope that Miss
Tilney had been in touch with Mr Ballard, saw the unlikeli-
hood of that, and forgot about the message too.

Rest was not easily available to Jacob Ballard when he
settled for the night in the room of the departed James
Morland. The night was silent except for the soft rustle of
breeze in the branches and the occasion shriek of a bird; it
was dark except for a sprinkling of stars; Jacob, to whom
the glow of furnaces was warmth, and the thud of the foundries the beat of his own heart, was dislocated; the result
was that, next day, he felt numb, as if wrapped in soft gauze
– it was too quiet here. There were noises – the yapping of
Xerxes, the stamp of hooves from the yard, a man shouting

137

– but they all melted, as it were, in the sunny silence. When Jacob fully woke, he would make plans – but at present all he could do – all he wanted to do – was to sit basking beside Charles in the garden.

'Tell me,' he began, trying to sound practical, 'will you be ready for school at Christmas?'

'I think so, but I am not sure that I want to go to school. I should have to direct my energies into too many things that would waste my time.'

'Indeed. So, what would not waste your time?'

'Reading. Preparing for Oxford. With a tutor.'

'At home? Your mother would insist.' To Jacob, his own voice sounded lazy. He heard Charles saying something about Mr Firth, who would not have to go back to college; Jacob asked:

'By the way how long are you and Mr Firth to stay here? Is his mother here permanently? She speaks as if she were.'

'I do not know. It seems as if we are all waiting for the Colonel, I do not know why. You see, he is an old friend of Mrs Firth.'

That did not afford Jacob much illumination. 'And that man – Firth's uncle – is to stay here until he has built a chapel? That will occupy a lifetime. I do not believe he has any idea of how to go about it.'

'Well,' said Charles uncertainly,' he knows where the old chapel stood; and he discovered the old well and the ice-house—'

'Much use. Look here, boy, you do understand that I am very angry with you for that stupid exploration you made?' His voice sounded merely sleepy. Charles said: 'Yes, I know, but you see I had to do something by myself.'

'No I do not see.' Involuntarily he added: 'Do you not care that I am angry? Are you not afraid of me at all?'

Charles appeared to ponder that. 'Yes, I am sometimes; I think you like me to be, sometimes.' The little imp was as cool as he was conciliating; it occurred to Jacob, in his

138

fanciful drowsiness, that he himself might sometimes be a little afraid of his son; the notion was strangely comforting.

Mrs Wight had seen to the sewing of black ribbons, knowing that the household staff ought to be in mourning – but, ought they? She and Mr Benson had conferred: It was strange that no tidings had been sent either to the Abbey or, as they had sent to ascertain, to the parsonage at Woodston. But it was more likely that a death would have been announced, than the non-occurrence of one; so Mrs Wight distributed the ribbons to be held in readiness, observing to Mr Benson that an atmosphere more mournful might well obtain at the Abbey. It was not that the household was indifferent to the probably bereaved Colonel but few of them knew Mrs Tilney, having met her only on the occasion of her one brief visit here, during which she had found fault with everything. The atmosphere had somehow deteriorated lately; Mrs Wight shook her head over the riotous hunting party in the cellars, the tendency of the outdoor staff to gather, watch and deride among themselves the enterprise of Mr Thorpe, and since Mr Morland had left, a lack of seriousness – now, with Master Charles's father strolling about, and the dog jumping about, and no lessons for Master Charles, there was even a kind of holiday air. No one expected the Colonel to appear; Mrs Wight guessed that it was a threat uttered by Mrs Firth, to keep everyone up to the mark, whatever that might be—Indeed, the spirit of the old General was apparently in eclipse.

'I wish though,' Mrs Wight sighed, 'that Miss Paulina might return.'

So did Charles. 'I wish, Papa, you could see Miss Tilney – she is so pretty; and she made us laugh – did she not, Mr Firth?'

'I suppose so,' replied Mr Firth in a tone of unutterable gloom. With an apparent effort he added: 'You were fond of Mr Morland too, Charles.'

'Yes, he was so kind. But not so gay; he is a clergyman. Mr Firth, do you think we might play with the bowls that Miss Tilney was showing us, when . . . when she had to go home? They are in the black cupboard in the drawing room. I saw them.'

Mrs Firth, who was present when Mr Ballard happened to be, said: 'Charles, I think it would be taking a great liberty, when Miss Tilney is away.'

'I am sure she would allow me. I am using her chairs and plates and everything in her absence, am I not? You see, Papa, it is a game I could play—'

'Probably you could, but I should wait, if I were you, until that right arm is strong again.'

'Oh, I had forgotten that.' Mrs Firth turned to Mr Ballard with a smile that said: He can forget his injuries when convenient. 'Well,' Charles urged, 'will not you and Mr Firth play, and then I could watch and learn?'

'Yes, shall we give him an exhibition, Firth? I suppose there is a bowling green?'

Roland and Charles exchanged glances; Roland said: 'Well, there is, but Mr Thorpe has dug a part of it up—'

'My brother is to blame for all the defects here; he has all but wrecked the place,' mentioned Mrs Firth. 'I am ashamed of him.'

Jacob Ballard went on: 'For practice, surely the lawn in front of the house would do well enough? Go and bring your bowls, Charles. Are you skilled in the game?' he asked Roland.

'No, I am afraid not. In fact I have never played.'

'But you will try, to oblige Mr Ballard,' his mother told him. 'I shall fetch my parasol; the sun is shining again.'

'Come, Firth, let us study the terrain,' Jacob said, before the young man could offer to fetch the parasol – had he meant to; he was still standing there gloomy.

Roland was, apart from his deprivation of Miss Tilney's society, in a state of painful embarrassment over his mother.

He could not understand nor countenance her behaviour, in assuming more and more the rôle of hostess – and her manner towards Mr Ballard was almost flirtatious. Mr Ballard did not seem to care – or notice; but what was she about, and what did she intend? Roland's own future was empty, but at least he could find employment, work and learn; his mother, when she left the Abbey, would go where? She should be worried, to be beginning again, in all probability, the series of visits and quarrels from which this summer had given reprieve; but she was serene and self-possessed; it puzzled him.

As he and Mr Ballard crossed the hall Mr Ballard asked: 'How long are you to be here?'

Roland, startled to have this echo of his thoughts, flinched. 'I do not know, sir. When do you wish Charles to go home?'

'I – and he, both – have written to mollify his mother. She will have to be patient; it was you I was thinking of. I agree with you that country air is better for Charles – I declare he has grown more than an inch . . . How if I were to set you and him up in lodgings – say, by the sea – and I would pay for you as much as I had expected to for school fees? But it would not be interesting for you, to be tied down to only one pupil.'

'Charles, you will believe, is interesting, sir. But it would not be fair to him, to be limited to one teacher – Nor could I accept payment so far in excess of my worth.'

'H'm,' commented Mr Ballard, not satisfied. 'Here he comes, now.'

Charles, in spite of the heavy net of bowls, seemed to his father to be limping less than usual. 'That left leg is growing stronger, do you feel?' he asked his son.

'I do, yes, sir. Do you know what Miss Tilney said? She said I might learn to ride, using a side saddle, like a lady—'

'Wearing a *skirt?*' came a horrified cry from Mrs Firth as she approached. The others laughed heartily.

141

'I doubt that, ma'am. They say, you know, that riding side saddle is more difficult than riding astride. Well, Charles, we shall have to find you a quiet steady pony to begin with.'

Mrs Firth as Charles laid out the bowls on the lawn stood by with a disapproving expression. She saw nothing amusing in that quite ridiculous suggestion of Miss Tilney's. No daughter of a dashing and accomplished horseman such as Captain Tilney should be able to lower herself to such foolery; he would be ashamed of her. This game of bowls promised to be a farce, as well; the spaniel had arrived on the scene and was trying to pick up a bowl in his mouth. How absurd. Furling her parasol she hit the beast sharply, whereat it twisted round and seized the tip of the parasol instead, bringing more laughter, and a piercing growl from the dog.

She was about to expostulate when hooves sounded from the direction of the main gate, and up the driveway came a carriage whose horses were neither quiet nor steady; they were at a gallop, the coachman as grim as if he could barely control them. He did however draw up, the carriage rocking and the horses blowing, in a scatter of gravel. A servant leapt down to open the door and guide to the step a hugely fat man with a scarlet face who without removing his hat or offering any greeting bellowed:

'Where is that d— man Thorpe?'

They all stared; only Roland said softly, as another figure climbed more slowly from the carriage:

'It is Miss Tilney.' He sounded incredulous, beyond delight.

15

If Paulina was glad on this occasion to arrive at the Abbey, it was simply because she had reached it alive. The journey had been appalling. She trusted Holcroft, the family coachman, but feared at moments that even he was driven to wildness by her father's temper. At home his bursts of rage had been bad enough, but once he had determined that he must set out for the Abbey and 'throw that d— rogue out' at once, speed had been reckless. Now, as she stood in the sunshine, she was trembling with exhaustion and could hardly stand.

The group on the lawn stood irresolute before the fury of the newcomer; no one – least of all Mrs Firth, who expected the dashing and handsome Captain Tilney, – recognised him; no one at first thought to notice that he and Paulina were not in mourning; it was only Roland, hurrying boldly forward, and urging: 'Miss Tilney – Please to take my arm—' who added as she gratefully did so:

'Your mother . . .?'

'She is improving – but slowly,' Paulina murmured. 'He would not let me write – He has been so angry . . . I am sorry, I am a little faint . . .' And she clung to his arm as he began to lead her indoors.

'Bring that rascal at once – and Benson – and the lot of them,' the Colonel was raging. A spaniel dog came rushing up to him and he kicked it aside. 'D— it, where is Brook? Bring me some wine. Get that dog away. Don't stand staring – Who *are* all these people?' He did not wish to be introduced but stamped off towards the house, where the Abbey staff had sprung to action with a promptitude that even the old General could not have evoked.

Brook was at the door bowing; messengers were speeding in all directions: Mr Benson and Mr Thorpe must be summoned, black ribbons were unnecessary, bedrooms must be prepared, the grooms must be hastened to see to those lathered horses, dinner must be augmented, someone must shut up that dog somewhere – and Mrs Wight was already approaching to greet Paulina and to soothe her and take off her bonnet. Roland yielded his precious charge and followed the others into the drawing room. Here the Colonel had flung himself on to a sofa and was still roaring for wine and for damnation upon all his idle and dishonest servants. He was regardless of the rest of the company, and these felt themselves mere spectators of what was to occur. There was a dread fascination too about the Colonel's very fury; his choler and obesity threatened himself – he might at any moment fall into an apoplexy – and if not, he was capable of murdering someone in this transport? He could not wait until the immediate culprits were before him, but continued to bellow:

'I will not have it, I swear to you, I will not have you all loafing about, eating your heads off, neglecting my property, and worse, knocking it about – Oh yes, you may think I am safely away in London, but I know what you have been up to behind my back – This *girl* has told me all about you and your mischief—'

Paulina, thus accusingly designated, lowered her eyes as she stood in the window apart from the others, afraid that they too would reproach her with treachery; but they pitied her, allowing that anything she told to this terrifying father must have been forced from her in virtual fear for her life.

144

There was no pause in his ranting until wine and Mr Benson were before him. Mr Benson was fittingly repentant that he had in the first place mentioned the shortcomings of the Abbey to John Thorpe; as he came through the cloister on his way here he had shuddered at the sight of the rubble left by Mr Thorpe's widening of the passage – and, Lord, when the Colonel sees the bowling green, he had begun to pray, his knees weakening. He stood before the Colonel speechless, and indeed given no opportunity to speak.

John Thorpe, who had been admiring his excavations on that same bowling green, was pleased to hear that the Colonel had arrived. 'Oh, splendid,' he exclaimed. 'Now he can see what I have done, so far, and I can explain my plans.' The footman who had come to warn him was ignored; John Thorpe swaggered into the drawing room dusting off his hands and crying: 'Good day to you, sir; I am glad you are come at last.'

This rendered even the Colonel briefly speechless. He breathed deeply, quaffed some wine, blew out his lips, and then said in a low and vicious tone:

'You will not for long be glad, you arrogant fool. I am come to stop your tricks and clap you in prison for your offences.'

John Thorpe laughed. 'Offences? What am I supposed to have done? Nothing but what you invited me to. I shall show you—'

The Colonel's voice rose again. 'Ay, you do not need to show me. I shall see for myself. I shall see for myself, sir, what damage you have done and you can hide nothing from me. I shall make you pay for every penny it will cost, to have that repaired by competent workmen.'

'Oh, as to that,' said John Thorpe, 'I am afraid my affairs are somewhat embarrassed at the moment. But I assure you the finished work will be rewarding—'

'It will not reward you. By G—, you have the cheek of the devil, standing there grinning and defying me.' At this he clapped down his glass with such violence that its stem snapped, and wiped with his wrist at the beads of sweat and fury on his brow.

The watchers, including the servants beyond the doorway, were compelled to admire John Thorpe's 'cheek' during this interview, whatever the rights and wrongs. Mrs Firth at the snapping of the wine glass felt as if a nerve within herself had snapped; she put her hand over her eyes to conceal the admission that those eyes forced upon her: This rampaging sot was not the handsome Captain Tilney. She was more than disappointed; she was angry; she loathed him. He had destroyed her life's dream.

'—And do not pretend I gave you any authority to touch one *stone* of the Abbey,' the Colonel was roaring. 'I do not even know you. I have perhaps seen you hanging about in Bath, telling your lies; but I have had and *will* have nothing to do with you once your offences are paid for. And paid for they will be. Bring me another glass, someone—'

Mrs Firth had left the room, unobserved. Paulina was leaning white-faced against the wainscot; Charles, fascinated as he was by this exhibition, seemed on the edge of being afraid for once; he stood half way behind a book case. His father stood beside him, rapt himself by the spectacle but feeling Charles should be spared it. It was Roland who moved, crossing to the cupboard where he knew glasses were kept, and taking out two glasses. He thus passed close to Paulina and whispered to her: 'In case of further breakage . . .'

He indicated the pair of glasses, slightly smiling. Paulina looked up at him; her eyes filled with tears but she too gave a gleam of a smile. Heaven knew it was not comical, any of this, but that Roland could imply a joke – could line up glasses for her father to smash – gave her enormous solace. She could not know how deeply Roland too had suffered from being embarrassed by a parent, but a sense of complicity gave them a moment's relief. Roland placed the glasses beside the Colonel and turned back to stand beside Paulina.

The Colonel's tirade was proceeding; he was promising that John Thorpe would be taken to court, and thence, if he were as poor as he claimed, to prison; he would be charged also with theft and wanton damage to property and illegal entry and lying – Even John Thorpe began to appear slight discomfited. It was now that Mrs Firth returned to the room. She held a scrap of paper in her hand; she advanced upon the sofa and said:

'Frederick.'

Startled, the Colonel paused in his raging. He stared at her before conceding: 'Who are *you*?'

'You will not remember,' Mrs Firth told him – with some truth; the dashing Captain had flirted with and discarded many young ladies in earlier times. 'But listen to this.' And she read in a firm voice from the scrap of paper, which looked to be a tradesman's bill:

' "I authorise John Thorpe to undertake what improvements are necessary at my estate. Frederick Tilney." '

'Give that to me!' shouted the Colonel; she did not. She turned to her brother and said coldly: 'It is as well that I kept this, is it not.'

'I had no idea that you had. Gad, what luck!'

'I did not intend to; somehow, I never took it out of my black carrying bag, which I do not often use,' Mrs Firth told him in a casual tone.

'It means nothing!' the Colonel protested, waving a hand. 'It is a forgery. It is not valid. It is only a vague statement. It does not authorise anything this rogue has done.'

Mrs Firth, glancing round, went over to Jacob Ballard and gave the note to him. 'Mr Ballard; you are a disinterested witness; you are the nearest thing to a lawyer that we have here. What do you think of this as a document?'

Jacob Ballard stepped forward and scanned the scrap of paper. 'This is a tailor's bill,' he announced, 'having been

147

paid, in Bath, on a date . . . Eleven months ago. On the back is the declaration that Mrs Firth read to us.' All at once, it seemed, his wits clouded by country air and quiet, revived. He turned to the Colonel.

'Shall we define the terms of this agreement?' He read it aloud, slowly. Then: 'You admit that the word "authorise" implies just that: To grant authority to?'

'I would never grant authority to such a man—'

'And "undertake" implies the beginning of a work, the acceptance of authority, with no promise that the work will be completed?'

'I thank heaven he has not completed anything—'

'And "improvements" commits the authorised person to no specific undertaking?'

'Stop this quibbling, man. Anyone knows what an improvement is and he has done d— little improving.'

'Nevertheless, I think a court of law might find the term too comprehensive to have legal force. And then: "necessary"; a court of law would possibly find that term unspecific, too.'

'What could be d— well necessary about a chapel? Do you know *that* is the stupid scheme the fool had in mind!'

'There again, a court of law could suppose that, since the original chapel was destroyed to the marring of the general layout of the abbey buildings, it should of necessity be replaced. Especially,' he added, 'if there were Roman Catholics in on the judgement. They are now emancipated in this country and—'

'You are a Jesuit yourself – You are proving nothing.'

'Exactly so. I am proving that you have no legal charge to lay upon Mr Thorpe. Whatever his offences, you have no valid claim to force their restitution upon him.'

'I can force what I choose upon him, and you too.'

'You will admit that this signature is yours?'

'Certainly not. He wrote it himself.'

Jacob Ballard turned to John Thorpe, who was listening

as baffled but not as angry as the Colonel. 'Were there any witnesses present when Colonel Tilney wrote this signature?'

'I do not suppose so; we were in the Club – Oh, wait: I remember that Michael Sturricott was there. I remember that he said the Colonel was crazy, to give me any authority – But that does not help.'

'Mr Sturricott may have been right, but the point at issue is that he saw the Colonel sign his name to this statement.'

'Michael Sturricott is crazy himself!' the Colonel roared.

'Quite so, but the same thing applies. Now, finally, do you accept, Colonel Tilney, that there is no mention at all here of money; that you did not offer payment to Mr Thorpe nor demand of him any payment for – for instance – incidental damage he might cause to the fabric, or for any materials he might require?'

'Oh, be quiet – Who are you to interfere? I shall have what I want, and my rights – By heaven you have muddled me – You are not as clever as you pretend – Give me that useless paper—' The Colonel tried to haul himself up from the sofa, clutching at the table beside him, which rocked under his weight and sent the two glasses and his bottles crashing to the parquet. Roland and Paulina exchanged less than a glance. Charles, who suffered no embarrassment on his parent's account, was listening with shining eyes. Mrs Firth stood with lips pursed, watching without pity as the Colonel relapsed on to the sofa with a face purpled by fury and effort.

'I shall call my own lawyer,' he panted. 'Give me that d— paper at once. It is *my* bill, on the other side, and you have no right to keep it from me—'

'It has been paid, and a receipt granted,' remarked Jacob, turning over the paper. 'If you require a receipt, you must apply to the tailor for a copy. Otherwise it can have no significance for you.'

'Let me have it; I must have it to keep!' cried John Thorpe.

'I agree, that it is likely to be of very great value to you. Perhaps, it might be safer to return it to Mrs Firth's keeping?'

'Let John have it; if he loses it, that is his loss,' said Mrs Firth indifferently. She had been satisfied by the rout of the Colonel but by now was finding the spectacle of his slobbering wrath merely disgusting.

'Thanks, Bella,' John Thorpe said, hastening to seize the significant document from Jacob Ballard; he chucked Charles under the chin, cried: 'Your father is splendid, is he not, Sweep!' and scuttled out of the room.

Charles said: 'I think what I will do, is to put that bill in an envelope and write on it large letters to say what it is, before Mr Thorpe crumples it up again or loses it. Shall I go and find him now, and do that?'

'It might be wise,' said Jacob Ballard.

'Oh, John can take care of himself,' Mrs Firth contributed. She cast a glance at the now recumbent Colonel and added, from force of recent habit: 'And now, shall I have dinner served?'

This caused Paulina some faint surprise; Roland dared to remonstrate:

'Mother, is that not for Miss Tilney to decide, now that she is here?'

'No – Please—' Paulina protested. At the sound of her voice the Colonel roused.

'Well, minx, are you satisfied now? You have seen your father cheated and tormented and exhausted, when he is already ill, and full of anxiety for your mother, whom you yourself have deserted, to bring me on this wild-goose chase half across the country . . . Where is my glass?'

'I am sorry, Papa. Would you not like some dinner?'

'To think of food at a time like this . . . Well, when I am rested, I suppose you will make me go round the place and examine the damage; but I am too tired . . . I shall go to bed. One thing I am determined on: take him to law or not,

150

I shall have that shabby villain Thorpe out of the place bag
and baggage before the day is over.'

'That might be wise,' Jacob Ballard remarked again. The
Colonel hauled himself upright again bawling:

'And you too, you pettifogging creeping false lawyer, and
all your friends – whoever they may be; I will not have the
place crowded with people I do not know and would d—
well not invite if I did. To hell with the lot of you.' With
which he fell back on the sofa, closed his eyes and began to
snore.

A subdued group met for dinner in the west parlour. John
Thorpe did not appear; it was to be hoped that he was
assembling his bag and baggage. When Charles came in to
describe the expedients he had made for the securing of
Mr Thorpe's valuable document, Mrs Firth asked:

'Was he packing?'

'I do not think so, ma'am. He was smoking his pipe and
looking at his plan of the chapel.'

'But he must go,' she exclaimed. 'He must see that.'

'I can see,' said Jacob Ballard, lightly, 'that we all must.'

Paulina gave a little gasp, and looked imploringly from
Mr Ballard to Roland, but there could be no discussion of
the Colonel and his menace in her presence. After a while
she said:

'If I had known – If I had understood from the first that
my father had not wanted to rebuild the chapel . . .' But it
was all too difficult; she now felt she had been as much to
blame for the difficulties as was John Thorpe. 'If only I had
written – My father decided so suddenly, to come . . .'

'The revelation of Mr Thorpe's activities was inevitable,'
Mr Ballard told her. 'And the time taken to remedy them
will be – and would have been – considerable. One good
thing has come about by your arrival: We are all very glad
to know that your mother is recovering from her illness.'

'But you did not think – You could not suppose – Oh, I

should have disobeyed – That is, I imagined that when no bad news was heard . . . I understand now what Mrs Wight meant, before dinner, when she spoke of there being no need of mourning.' Mrs Wight, her attention preoccupied, had made one small error, in leaving a bundle of the retrieved black ribbons on the table of the housekeeper's room; since Paulina was last here, no one but the maids had been in the habit of entering there.

Paulina could eat nothing; Roland, from sympathy, could find no appetite; and at this point, it was Mrs Firth who laid down her spoon, distracted by the recollection that she would not, even yesterday, have joined in Mr Ballard's gladness that Mrs Tilney had not died.

In her revulsion from the obnoxious Colonel and her pleasure in defeating his designs on her brother, she had overlooked the fact that her handsome Captain Tilney no longer existed. For over twenty years, she had kept him in her heart, and she had overlooked too the possibility that he would have aged – more, that he could have grown so fat and ugly. It was unbearable. She would not even have mourned for him, so grotesque was his present incarnation – Or rather, she could not accept the new emptiness of her heart. It was too cruel. She was truly alone in the world, bereft even of her dream. She felt her face pale and her breath check; she felt the others should have observed her anguish, but Mr Ballard was still speaking to Miss Tilney – still on the topic of her mother's illness:

'. . . Then you and your father are still anxious, at leaving her alone; he will not wish to tarry here long?'

'But if he goes,' murmured Paulina, 'he will take me with him.'

'Then,' remarked Charles in his bright childish voice, 'there will be *none* of us here!'

Mrs Firth, annoyed by his prattle, said: 'Charles; are you feeding that dog at the table?'

He straightened, saying: 'Well, it was *under* the table, ma'am – Only a piece of apple peel—'

'Dogs should not eat apple peel, and you should not be impudent.'

Now it was Miss Tilney who roused herself, looking about as if recollecting: 'But who else was here . . . Oh, where is Uncle James? I had forgotten. I had hoped to see him.'

'He went back to Woodston,' Roland told her. 'It was some time ago; I do not know why he left.'

Nor, now, did Mrs Firth. She did not see how, among all the recent commotions and arrivals, she had come to forget him. She felt that she had missed him more than she admitted; he had been so kind, so dignified, so gentlemanly – so calm, and *thin*. She rose from the table.

'I am almost overcome by all the strain I have undergone; if you will excuse me, I have letters to write.'

As the footman opened the door for her, rumblings of snores could be heard along the corridor from the drawing room. Mrs Firth almost ran all the way up the stairs to escape the noise.

Alone in her room Mrs Firth compelled herself to recognise that she was again alone in the world. She gazed out of the window at the sunny landscape of the Abbey that she loved so much – at the rose gardens and rippling aspens, and the distant boughs of the orchards where the apples were reddening – and knew she must bid farewell to this kingdom that had promised to be hers. She thought herself a woman of fine sentiments, and sentimental she was when she had the leisure for it; but at present her instinct for survival was predominant.

John would go; for all his swagger he secretly knew when he was beaten, and besides, he had been long enough on a task he also knew to be beyond his abilities. Mr Ballard would go, taking Roland and Charles back to Birmingham. The Colonel and his daughter would go, back to London and the undying Mrs Tilney. It was strange, Mrs Firth mused, how history repeated itself; all those years ago, she had undervalued James for a short time and been tempted by the specious charm of Captain Tilney – but she had been young and innocent, and ignorant of the perfidy of men. Now she had learnt wisdom and could divine her own true feelings. She took up her pen.

My dear James
For so I may address you, for the sake of old times? I have been hoping to hear from you but must be improper enough to write to you first, to share our pleasure here on the recovery of Mrs Tilney. You will understand how much I was suffering on her account when we heard of her illness; if I was cool in my manner, it was only to spare you my unhappiness. Did I not suspect a trace of reserve too in your manner? You must not be aloof with me. You and I have much in common and we must repair the slight rift between us. I cannot think what caused it. Miss Tilney has been remiss in correspondence and we have had little news lately; I would be glad to know how they all do at Woodston and how the work on your London house goes ahead. I shall soon be quitting the Abbey and hope to hear from you before I do, because where I shall be going I do not yet know. However, I have been home-less before, and can bear it with fortitude, tho' life is empty without a companion. I think of you each time I look at the little pearl cross you admired – but more than that survives of our long association!
Yours in all gratitude for your friendship,
Isabella Firth.

He was probably still at Woodston since he was not due in London till Advent; the letter should soon reach him. She sealed it, for privacy, and without pausing to admire the view from her window.

16

As the evening drew on, the Colonel became an embarrassment in another fashion: His snores had ceased and he had fallen into a profound slumber; was he to be woken? How was he to be taken to bed? Brook the butler, entering the west parlour where the company had been sitting since the table was cleared in order to leave the Colonel undisturbed, indicated as politely as he could that if the Colonel woke there might be a revival of his wrath, but that if he did not, it was beyond the power of anyone to carry him up the stairs.

Paulina said: 'It would be a pity to wake him; he needs the rest.'

So do we all, thought both Brook and Jacob Ballard, who was sitting beside Paulina. Brook went on:

'If I may suggest it, Miss Paulina, since the Colonel has not brought his valet, one of the footmen and I could remove his boots and cravat, and lay a quilt over him; and someone could be at hand in case he requires attention in the night.'

In a decided tone Jacob Ballard said: 'Yes, that would be the best plan. Do you agree, Miss Tilney?'

Paulina agreed, not ungratefully. She now found her father pitiful – pathetic in his sleep as in his tantrums; she was grateful again that Mr Ballard called after Brook:

'If you need any help, call me.'

There was authority in his voice; Brook turned back to give him a nod of acknowledgement. The household, having seen the Colonel bested by this gentleman already today, was glad of the gentleman's presence. And Paulina, as Brook left, said:

'Mr Ballard, I am sorry that you had to witness scenes today that were no concern of yours, but I have been glad of your support. I do not think, you know, that my father truly wished you to leave the Abbey at once. But I would not detain you . . . Perhaps, tomorrow . . .'

She did not know what she wished for tomorrow. Jacob Ballard assured her:

'Tomorrow, I can stay or go, as I am best advised. It seemed your father did not wish to remain for long here? If Mr Thorpe keeps out of his sight – or, better, leaves – your father may set off early?'

'He meant to. He of course does not want to be long away from my mother. But Holcroft says that our horses must have a full day's rest before facing another journey like today's.'

Jacob Ballard forbore to mention that a railway train would require no such indulgence. He pointed out: 'Your father too might be in need of further rest. We shall see how he is, when he wakes. A few days of quiet and country air could restore him.'

'Yes, but he does not care for the country.'

Nor do I, Jacob also forbore to mention. But it had on me a stultifying effect, did it not, that this Colonel could well do with. 'Well; we shall see what the day brings. – Mr Firth: do you wish to speak to me? I know what it must be: Your letter. I have it here – It has been all day in my pocket.'

He rose and crossed the room to Roland, who had been observing with an anxious air this colloquy between Mr Ballard and Miss Tilney. But it was not his letter that had been on his mind; as the two of them met in the window recess, the letter went straight from Jacob Ballard's hand into his own pocket as he began:

'Sir – I have been wondering – If you were to go home and to take Charles with you – And if the Colonel were to stay – could it possibly be arranged for me to stay behind too? For a little while? My mother speaks of leaving too, and I might – though I am useless – be able to be of some help to – to Miss Tilney . . .'

Jacob clapped him on the shoulder. 'Why, that is a very gallant suggestion. Do not blush! I am sure the lady does not require you to be useful – only to bear her company. And you may do that with my blessing, whether Charles and I go home or not.'

Roland, blushing more deeply, glanced with horror across the room to see whether Miss Tilney had overheard any of that; but she was turning to Brook, who had appeared in the doorway to announce:

'The Colonel is settled and still fast asleep, Miss Tilney.'

If the servants' dining room had found high comedy in the notion of its master sleeping on the sofa, no one there would let Miss Paulina suspect that. Mrs Wight decided that it was for the family and its guests to solve their own affairs, and that breakfast would be served tomorrow quite as usual.

Before breakfast was served next morning John Thorpe pounded at Mrs Firth's door and entered in buoyant spirits, smoking his pipe.

'Good morning, my dear—'

'John, if you fill the house with that foul smoke it will warn the Colonel that you are still here.'

'Oh, what do I care for that old sot,' declared John Thorpe, who had ascertained that the Colonel was still asleep on his sofa. 'Listen: I have decided to leave today—'

'*You* have decided?'

'—Since my plans have been frustrated by that old besom who will not let me knock down one wall of her useless scullery, or whatever it is – And since our worthy Colonel is so ungrateful for all my endeavours – So, farewell for the present—'

'Farewell for longer than that, I hope.'

'Do not be so unfriendly! I have come to you with a most friendly intention, and an offer. By the way I am glad you happened to keep that piece of paper old Fatty signed, and which young Sweep has stitched inside the lining of my best coat. So this is what I offer: You may come to my house in Bristol when you are flung out of the Abbey. Now is not that a generous and brotherly kindness?'

'I wonder that even you can think so. That house is but half finished, uncomfortable and draughty, and surrounded by tradesmen and debtors and neighbours all eager to fling you out of it.'

'Oh, nonsense. They will have tired of waiting by now – And they had no complaint against me; I may owe a sovereign or two, but all that will soon be settled. Your charming manner will assist—'

'And my money, you imply; but you know I have none.'

'Why should you take such a bitter view of my motives?' he asked, in a tone of deep injury.

'Because I know you. Now, John, do go, before you cause any more trouble; and take off your boots and tiptoe down the stairs lest you wake your ungrateful Colonel.'

Shaking his head at the ingratitude of yet another friend, John left; he swaggered down the stairs, but when Charles met him in the hall and cried: 'Good morning, Mr Thorpe—' John leapt into the air and pressed a finger to his lips, recovering in time however to whisper:

'Hush, shrimp – our host is still sleeping . . .'

Colonel Tilney slept on, until John Thorpe had departed and breakfast was finished. The concern then was: Should he be woken? Had he slept too long?

He had; much as he needed rest, his repose had not been

comfortable and at some incidental sound – the slam of a distant door or a yap from Xerxes – he opened his eyes unwillingly and found himself in pain of every kind: His neck was stiff, his legs ached, his whole frame was cramped. He could not move. At first he could not cry out – his voice was a dry croak. He knew himself very ill.

This condition of the Colonel's did not entirely surprise Brook or the footman who presently braced arms behind him and persuaded him, groaning, to climb the stairs. It was the sight of Miss Paulina's white face that made Brook ask Mr Ballard:

'Do you think the doctor should be called, sir?'

'It might be a precaution.'

The doctor arrived, and diagnosed muscle cramp, fatigue and obesity; his prescription, as he did not elaborate on these symptoms to his patient, was: 'You must rest.'

'By G—, have I not rested these many hours and grown the worse for it?' the Colonel croaked; but his bed was soft and a nightgown wonderfully soothing; he fell asleep again.

An interval of peace supervened. The housemaids began their work – glancing in at the door of the breakfast room, wincing at the confusion therein and closing the door again – and Jacob Ballard went to the stables to confer with his own coachman about readiness for possible departure; Charles and Xerxes accompanied him; Mrs Firth was in her room, unpicking a frill of lace that she had frivolously sewn on to her grey gown. Roland and Paulina were left to walk in the shrubbery, as she preferred the shade; they averted their eyes from the ragged gap in the yew hedge; to Paulina, the Abbey this morning was as charming as it had ever been.

Roland was so much delighted to be alone with her that he could think of nothing in the world to talk to her about. When he had considered the weather and the world news but found nothing to say about either, it was she who asked:

'What has Charles been up to? How did he bruise his face and hurt his one good arm?'

159

'Oh . . . You were not here . . . Of course,' and he could relate the tale of Charles's adventures, which horrified but amused her. Then he could inquire about her mother, and deduce from her reply – and from his first acquaintance with her father – how difficult a time she and her sister had been passing in London. Hesitantly she added: 'I believe my father decided so suddenly to come to the Abbey because my mother became – She is easily upset just now – She felt him impatient with her, and told him he was delaying her recovery; and I feel perhaps they may be the better for a little while apart. If he will stay here, it should do him good. Neither of us is truly necessary to my mother just now, whatever he says – And,' she distracted herself from this implied contradiction of her father, 'my sister is I hope happy, with her friends by the sea.'

After struggling for a felicitous expression of his thought but seeing the end of the shrubbery path all too near, Roland broke out: 'I hope you too are happy among friends, here.'

She replied: 'Mr Ballard has been so kind, has he not. And I am always happy to be at the Abbey . . .' They were at the limit of the path; she turned, and met his gaze – beseeching and tender; he quickly blinked his eyes but hers would not let them go; she too was both shy and imploring. They stood without moving for one endless moment. When they turned back up the shrubbery they found themselves hand in hand, and walking in no hurry at all.

The grey gown looked very drab without the lace. Mrs Firth supposed that she need not wear it until she was with James again, but she put away her workbox in some annoyance, which was increased when, downstairs, she met her son Roland entering from the garden, pink-faced and pleased with himself.

'Where have you been?' she demanded.

'In the shrubbery, with Miss Tilney.'

'Alone? My dear Roland, you must have some sense of conduct. Particularly at a time like this, with her mother and father so ill, Miss Tilney should be above reproach and not show herself indecorous. Her behaviour is as improper as yours.'

Roland had his foot on the lowest stair; he swung back to say: 'She is not in the least indecorous or improper!'

'You are defying my judgement?'

'Yes.'

'Then you will not disobey my orders and do anything so foolish as to propose marriage. You know how impossible that is – And you are a fool to chase after the first girl you meet. You will not dare to speak to her.'

'I dare not, but I will.'

His mother fixed him in a glacial gaze. Quietly she said: 'Go back to Birmingham with your Ballards and do not let me see you again.'

She meant to see him again only when she had James to share with her the gift of Christian forgiveness. Roland, not answering her, nor caring what she meant, went up to his room between rage and rapture, flung off his boots and coat and threw himself along his bed. Marry her or not, he felt that his love for Miss Tilney was the safe and precious treasure of his life; the oyster in his pearl – or the other way about? His poetic paradox was unresolved by a tap at the door; to his call, Charles and the dog entered.

'Mr Firth – Are you not well? I am sorry—'

'No . . . Come in.'

Charles studied his tutor with some doubt. 'But you are throwing your things about like Mr Thorpe. Did he tell you that I sewed my envelope into his coat? You see how good my right hand is now? – Only he threaded the needle for me. I wish he had not gone. – Xerxes, what are you chewing? Here – Good boy. Mr Firth, this is a letter that fell out of your pocket – Shall I have to sew for you too?'

The letter whose adventures had ended almost in its being

161

eaten by a dog had not been improved by its delay. Roland tried to make out the re-directions – Dellingham. Oxford, and Birmingham – smudged with rain and travel. 'Read it to me, Charles, if you can open it with your excellent right hand; it is a bill, I think; not a personal letter.'

Charles took Roland's pen knife and slit the grubby envelope. 'It is from some firm . . . of solicitors.' As Roland wearily sighed, Charles sat on the foot of the bed and cleared his throat. 'It is difficult to understand . . . and there are numbers – Well, these people, MacVitie, Merchison and Sons, say Dear Sir, We now have to inform you that as you will reach your majority on your twenty-first birthday on the seventh day of next month – Did you have a birthday, sir? While we were at the Abbey – Yes, I see, from these dates – You could have told me?'

'I forgot. Read on. What do they want from me?'

'—Yes. "The trust established on the day of your birth by Mr Hamish McTaggart Firth of fifteen Moray Crescent Glasgow will reach maturity and we would be obliged if you could make communication with us in order to register your acceptance of the accumulated amount and to sign the relevant documents. The trustees were as afore instituted by the same Hamish McTaggart Firth appointed from the administrators of the Regent Merchant Banking and Shipping Company in which Company the initial moneys were invested. The total accrued amount now at your disposal we now certify as . . . Twenty seven" – Wait I cannot speak this number—'

'Twenty seven pounds?' prompted Roland.

'Oh no. "Twenty seven *thousand* eight hundred and forty two pounds".'

'Do not be careless, Charles. Read it again.'

'No, that is what it says. Except that there are some more figures, about what investments earned how much – and "Less Legal Fees" – but that is only little figures. Oh, sir, how rich you will be! Is that not exciting? To think, Xerxes might have chewed up all those thousands of pounds—'

Roland, sitting up, studied the letter. 'Who would institute anything on the day of my birth? I never heard of a Hamish what-is-it Firth – he might be a relation, but I think these lawyers have mixed me up with someone else.'

'My Papa would explain it, sir,' said Charles simply.

In equal faith, Roland put on his boots and they went down to the drawing room where, with the Colonel's bedding and broken glass cleared away, Mr Ballard sat with Mrs Firth. Roland would have preferred not to encounter his mother again so soon after their meeting in the hall, but she might be able to explain the letter too; and Charles was already saying:

'Papa, Mr Firth does not think this letter should have been sent to him, but perhaps to someone else named Firth?'

Jacob Ballard took the letter and read it, his brows rising. 'It is addressed correctly enough, if your second name is Reginald?'

'I am afraid so – I normally conceal it.'

'But not from these people who also know your date of birth and have kept count of the years. Who was Hamish McTaggart Firth?'

From Mrs Firth, who had closed her eyes, came a half scream of anguish. 'That was the name of that cruel and miserly man, my husband's father.'

'Then,' said Jacob Ballard unmoved by her outcry, 'he was your paternal grandfather, Mr Firth. I confess I do not think it either cruel of him, or miserly, to make provision for a grandchild as soon as he knew of the birth. You understand that to place the money in trust until you were of age meant that you could not have it until then; and it seems that the trustees have handled the capital well, because meanwhile it has increased in value by almost one third.'

'But why did no one tell me?' exclaimed Roland.

163

'No one told me – which is more serious!' Mrs Firth cried. 'Show me that letter!' She scanned it as Jacob Ballard inquired:

'Is it possible that no one was told? This Mr Hamish Firth may have had his reasons.'

'I am sure he would think so. He had a hard, mercenary nature. He would not give money to his own son – my husband – yet he hid it away for a baby he did not even *see*.'

'How old were you, Mr Firth, when your grandfather died?'

'I did not know that he had died, sir – I knew nothing of him.'

'It was I,' supplied Mrs Firth with some passion, 'who chose to know nothing of that family. They cast off my husband with no mercy – they abandoned him to poverty – *he* had nothing in his father's will, and I have suffered ever since for that.'

Jacob Ballard smiled at Roland. 'You should be all the more grateful, it seems, to your grandfather, that he favoured your cradle in preference to the others of your family.'

'In preference to *me*, you are implying?' Mrs Firth took up sharply. 'That money is due to me – for all the expense I have been at, to bring up my child without help.'

'However that may have been,' said Jacob Ballard in a grave and impersonal tone, 'this legacy is wholly and entirely at the disposal of Roland Reginald Firth, as was his grandfather's wish.'

'But Roland might have turned out as profligate as his f— That is, he is not capable of handling so much money.'

'That was a risk his grandfather was prepared to take.'

'It is absurd, Roland, remember what you owe to me and to others – To your Uncle George. You must be generous and consult your elders. You are not fit to deal with such wealth . . .'

Roland received a measuring glance from Mr Ballard

which reminded him that he had perhaps relied too much so far on that member of his 'elders'. He must show Mr Ballard his gratitude. For the second time in an hour he defied his mother, by saying gently but resolutely:

'Mama dear, I am of age now, and I must honour my grandfather's intentions by deciding for myself, and by myself, what is to be done with his legacy. I will tell you what I decide, and hope you will approve of it.'

Charles, closely attending, thought to himself: It is strange that becoming a year older can make Mr Firth taller and more manly, all at once. Perhaps when I am twenty-one the same thing will happen to me.

17

After a very few days the Colonel admitted that being ill was a tedious affair. He sent for his clothes and trod quite steadily downstairs, roaring: 'Paulina!' She came running from the housekeeper's room to find him standing in the hall.

'Where is everyone?' he asked, as if puzzled.

'Mr Ballard and Charles are gone to Birmingham, Papa, and Mr Firth has had to go to Glasgow on some business.' She did not add that, when he had mollified his wife, Mr Ballard was to seek out lodgings by the sea where his son and Mr Firth might spend some time – perhaps at Cromer, whither Miss Tilney might go to visit her sister who was staying with her friends the Harringtons. The ingenuity of Roland and Paulina in such arrangements was exceeded only by their optimism; they knew they would marry; otherwise their future was a happy blank. 'Mr Thorpe went, of course,' Paulina continued. A glint of rage shone in the Colonel's eye as he made for the drawing room. 'And Mrs Firth is still here,' Paulina added, not certain that her father was still listening. He gave a grunt that indicated nothing; indeed he had no idea who Mrs Firth might be.

Mrs Firth was still here, still waiting for a reply from James to her letter, and struggling to adjust her ideas of her son now that he was to be accoutred with money. In spite of herself – and in accordance with her own scale of values – she could not help regarding him with something like respect. She knew that he would make her an allowance from his new wealth but hesitated to ask – much less to demand. He had always been a good obedient boy, and was a man who would acknowledge what was due to his mother. When these tiresome affairs of his were settled he could leave his post as tutor and spend some time in London; he would now be no burden to James.

As she stood at the top of the stairs she heard the sound of hooves below, and of arrival. Touching the seed pearl cross at her throat and crossing to a window she saw a figure in dark clerical hat handing the reins of his horse to a footman; she descended with a smile that faded as, entering the drawing room, she found a stranger – stockier than James, but a fine-looking man – standing with his back to the fireplace, swinging his riding whip and addressing Colonel Tilney:

'. . . So we had trouble enough, and then the children had what we thought was scarlet fever – No, do not flinch, Frederick, it was but nettle rash – I wish I could have come sooner, for I hear peculiar stories of what has been happening here.' He broke off to bow to Mrs Firth; it was Paulina who came forward:

'Mrs Firth, this is my Uncle Henry, from Woodston.'

'Ma'am . . . I must look round to see that the damage is not serious. I noticed the yew hedge as I rode up – Will it be necessary to cut the entire thing down?'

'Gad, I do not care. I do not care what becomes of this whole place,' the Colonel grumbled. His brother gave him a tolerant smile, remarking: 'You do not look too fit yourself; but I am mightily glad that Lauretta is recovering. Will you be going home soon, since you care nothing for the Abbey?'

'As soon as possible, on my oath; let it all tumble down.'

Paulina said: 'Uncle, the repair work has begun already; the masons have mended the corner wall of the cloister.'

167

'I am reassured. We should be glad to have you at Woodston again, my dear; your visit was too short. Oh, and another trouble we have had,' he went on turning to the Colonel, 'was that James came back to us from here in a serious state of depression. I know he is no sunbeam at any time, but he has been moping there, telling us he is a failure and has lost his vocation. Well, that was nonsense, but we were worried, I can tell you. I told him that the best thing for him would be a change of scene and perhaps temporary occupation, until he goes to London – but no. I had thought of the Brothers of Good Endeavour – You know, that Anglican order that does so well for the seamen in south Wales—'

'No I do not *know*,' interrupted the Colonel, scowling.

'Yes?' at the same moment Mrs Firth cried in sudden alarm.

'You do, ma'am? James has always admired them. Well, just a couple of days ago he received a letter – he did not say what was in it, but it stirred him up! He packed his box and was off to Wales immediately, full of endeavour; I have never known him in such a hurry. So that is one less trouble in our house. Well, and I am in a hurry too; I must be at the deanery in half an hour. My dear Paulina, try to come to us at Woodston? Frederick, look to yourself – and to dear Lauretta. I am sorry not to see your chapel rising, when I had so kindly lent you my unhelpful picture, but with John Thorpe engaged in the work I could not expect much; I am surprised you dealt at all with him. Shall I see you in Bath this year?' He kissed Paulina, bowed to Mrs Firth and was gone; they heard his horse cantering busily off.

Mrs Firth went slowly up the stairs, quite dazed by this desertion of James's. There was no end to the frustrations and humiliations that fate loaded upon her. At the head of the stairs she permitted herself to lean on the window sill with her hands over her face, in a posture of agony and despair. The cuff of her sleeve caught in the chain of the seed pearl cross, whose catch was still broken; Mrs Firth tore off the cross and hurled it into the bushes below the window. The gesture awoke a little spirit in her and she could begin to seek someone to blame for her plight.

She had not far to seek. Both – all, counting her husband – the men she had given her heart to had betrayed her and proved unworthy. Horace with his gambling – Captain Tilney by growing fat and selfish – and, yes, James was selfish too; he was weak and hesitant; he dared not face her and risk encountering his true feelings – which in any case were not true; he was jealous and cowardly – and what was he about, to depart so hurriedly? Mrs Firth had never heard that there were seamen in south Wales.

Here, then, she was again, alone in the world. It did not bear thinking of. Yet, now, there was some comfort: Roland. She need not care for any of these Tilneys and Morlands, now that she had a good son to be a refuge and support. His thousands of pounds cushioned her mind and soothed her. She turned to go to her room but a voice from the stairs detained her.

'Mrs Firth . . .?' It was soft and persuasive and belonged of course to the Tilney girl; impatient, Mrs Firth waited.

'. . . Excuse me. My father has now resolved to go back to London tomorrow, and I shall have to go with him. If I may ask: What are your own plans?'

Ah, the hussy is daring to fling me out, at last, Mrs Firth thought; but the hussy was continuing: 'I wondered whether it would please you to accompany us? We could set you down anywhere in town; and since my father is in no special haste and not yet feeling too well, the journey will be . . . quieter than ours on the way down here.'

The offer of a free ride was offset by the recollection that money need not be so significant an issue now that Roland was able to pay; but with the recollection of Roland came the daunting admission that he and this girl fancied themselves in love. Mrs Firth's new regard for her son did not extend so far as to concede him control of his personal life. It was an absurd idea – the Colonel would refuse consent, and so would she; though what use was the refusal from a frail and solitary woman? It struck Mrs Firth as the girl stood there waiting to hear of Mrs Firth's plans, that what was intolerable about her was that she was so culpably, offensively *young*, with her shining hair and delicate dimples. With one push, Mrs Firth could have sent her hurtling down the stairs. But fortunately for good sense (and for Paulina's neck) a part of Mrs Firth's mind was pursuing a parallel course. One had to admit that young people did marry, and this girl was presentable, and rich; moreover she was too young to know her own mind – some handsome Captain Tilney of this era might intervene; Mrs Firth remembered what it was like to be innocent and impressionable. She would warn Roland of that, as a beginning. Meanwhile of course, travel plans. After swift reflection she said graciously:

'You may take me as far as the coaching station here. Then I shall make my way to my sister's. I need be no further beholden to you. Send a maid to see to my packing, if you please.'

She would go to Anne, who would be delighted to hear of Roland's good fortune; and it would be interesting to know what George had to say; would he expect Roland to repay all that had been spent on his education? There was promise of a lively quarrel on that account.

In her room, Mrs Firth surveyed her assorted dresses – drab grey, worn slippers, limp muslins – and almost decided to have nothing packed. She must throw behind her all that was left of this grievous and painful summer. She swore to herself that she would never, never see this terrible Abbey again.

Nor did she. As the years passed, the Reverend Roland Firth and his family passed much happy time at the Abbey; but if they wished to see Mrs Firth they must seek her at one of the fashionable watering-places or resorts at which she, willingly provided for by him, lived pleasantly enough, ever in wait for a husband.